SWIMMING

WITH

STRANGERS

SWIMMING

WITH

STRANGERS

STORIES

KIRSTEN SUNDBERG LUNSTRUM

CHRONICLE BOOKS
SAN FRANCISCO

This is a work of fiction. Names, places, characters, and
incidents are products of the author's imagination or are
used fictionally.

Some of the stories in this book were previously published
in somewhat different form: "The Drowning" in *Willow
Springs*, "The Nursery" in *The American Scholar*, and
"Familial Kindness" in *One Story*. "The Nursery" also
appears in *The PEN/O. Henry Prize Stories 2009*.

Library of Congress Cataloging-in-Publication Data:

Lunstrum, Kirsten Sundberg, 1979-
  Swimming with strangers : stories / Kirsten Sundberg Lunstrum.
    p. cm.
  ISBN 978-0-8118-6076-5
  I. Title.

PS3612.U56S95 2008
813'.6--dc22

                        2008013340

Manufactured in Canada
Cover and interior design by Andrew D. Schapiro

10 9 8 7 6 5 4 3 2 1

Chronicle Books LLC
680 Second Street
San Francisco, California 94107

www.chroniclebooks.com

FOR MY PARENTS.

AND FOR FINN, WHO HAS MADE
EVERYTHING MORE BEAUTIFUL.

CONTENTS

ISLANDS

IT WAS ELLEN'S IDEA to spend the holiday on the island. She liked the idea of weather—the fog, the heavy feel of the salt-weighted sea air, as if they were in a mystery book—*Rebecca* maybe—or a romance.

They arrived at the resort mid-morning on December 30, though *resort* seemed an inappropriate word for what looked to Loren more like a campground—a string of hastily built shanties on the western side of Orcas Island, some of them newer than others, each rain-wet and leaning slightly toward the gray water of Puget Sound. Their cabin was the last on the short beach, a one-bedroom with shake siding and a low porch. The stoop had often been submerged beneath the lip of a high tide, so that the boards of the crude steps had taken on the look of driftwood, rubbed smooth and white when dry. Inside, the front door opened onto a large kitchen and a sitting room, the walls wood-paneled and the slats of the pine floor gritty with sand tracked in on the last vacationers' feet. There was a slumping couch in one corner, a coffee table on spindle legs, and a squat wood-burning stove that Loren struggled to get going, kneeling in front of it, blowing his breath into the stove's belly to encourage the impossibly damp kindling to light.

"Don't fuss it," Ellen said, her voice pleasant and unbothered. She laid a hand against his back briefly as she passed into the bedroom, the stack of bed linens she'd brought from home in her arms.

Ellen had packed for them both, and now the cabin was cluttered with their winter sweaters and rain slickers and boots, several bags of dry-goods groceries and water bottles and wine, books and games and a suitcase of housewares. She'd packed sheets and towels, a wool afghan that seemed to have already absorbed the air's humidity and so smelled to Loren like a wet animal, four or five braided throw rugs that she scattered throughout the cabin to take up the sand.

When Loren saw her unloading the suitcases, hanging their clothes in the bedroom closet and setting their toiletries in order in the bathroom medicine chest, he could think only of having to pack it all away again in five days, of piling each blanket and unopened bottle of wine back into the trunk of their car. *What do we need with all this?* he wanted to ask her. But their belongings seemed to content his wife, to provide her a sense of purpose. She moved about the cabin settling in, straightening the towels in the bathroom and folding the afghan over the back of the couch. She gathered the rugs and carried them to the porch, where she beat them against the railing, humming, a shimmer of dust carried from home loosening from the rugs' weave as she shook them out. She planned to wake before Loren each morning, to sweep the front room, to start a pot of coffee in the metal percolator, to walk the beach in her mucking boots and heavy sweater before the sun was completely up. Out here, it seemed, she was all industry, all good humor and rosy mood, the color up in her cheeks again and her voice bright.

"Don't you want to walk with me?" she asked once she had finished with her homemaking—had made the bed and wiped out the basin of the sink, which the last visitors had left sandy; once Loren had stacked the five bundles of firewood they'd ferried over from the mainland into a neat pyramid beside the woodstove. "There's sun today, Loren," she said, pulling her scarf from the peg near the door. "We should make use of it before it passes." She wrapped the blue scarf around her neck and pulled a hat down over her short gray hair. Her face had become slightly pinched since she'd lost all her weight, and her skin already had the thin, pink, tissue-paper look of old age. Her eyes were the same as when he'd met her, though, and Loren noted how clear and blue they were at this moment, as she stood working her mittens over her hands, bundled and waiting for him to join her.

"You go," he said. "I'll keep the fire."

He gave her time to get a distance from the cabin and then went to the window. There was sun, and it cast a glare on the water outside and beamed into the cabin through the window glass, lighting a slant square on the pine planks of the floor. The ledge was warm when he put his hands to it. Down the beach, Ellen walked at a quick pace and then slowed, and then stopped altogether and bent down, hands to knees, catching her breath. He could not see her face, only the blue scarf coming loose at her neck, tugged like a kite tail by the wind. Above her, the wind rushed high, thin clouds across the sky, so that the sunlight flickered on the beach, and the water seemed one moment too bright to look at, too dull the next. Loren stood at the window and watched until she stood straight again and kept walking, slower now, stooping every few feet to pick up a clot of kelp, a piece of driftwood, something small that she put into her pocket.

Sometimes she looked sick to him still—a fragile version of herself. When she bent down to pick up the kelp, for instance—an unsteady step back and then forward again, a hand grasping the air in that second of unbalance. These moments stopped him. He nearly opened the window to call to her.

He wished they had stayed home.

He had protested when she first brought up the idea of a holiday getaway. "I'm fine now," Ellen had insisted, though, peevish with his concern. "We should celebrate. I've been pardoned. Remitted." She thumped her chest with both fists, Jane of the Jungle, and smiled. "Please, Loren, stop fretting me."

She made the reservations then, and he didn't say any more, yet he felt now as he'd expected he would, watching her through the window as she stood at the waterline. Not celebratory, not excused, but obliged. Bound.

On the beach there was a moment of sunlight, the water green again, then brown, the thick black bodies of the other islands backlit and then shadowed. Loren watched his wife picking along the sand, the pockets of her sweaters full at her thighs and bulging with the treasures she'd collected on her walk, the sun on her shoulders. He turned away from the window and toward the stove, where he added another log, another fistful of rumpled newsprint.

It was late afternoon when the young couple pulled up in front of the cabin next door and got out of their little pickup truck—a rumpled-looking young man with a mop of curly hair in serious need of a cut, and a girl. She was blonde, and at the moment Loren looked up from his reading, she shifted her weight—hip to hip—to bump shut her door, and then shrugged her long braids over her shoulder so that the round curve of her cheek was visible for an instant before she turned her back again.

Ellen was on the porch reading, her hat low over her ears and a mug of hot tea balanced on the railing within reach of her lawn chair, but she put her book down when she saw the couple arrive, stood up, and waved hello. "We have neighbors," she called to him through the window. And then to the couple: "Hello, neighbors!"

It was ridiculous to sit outside, Loren thought, when he had spent the morning building up the fire inside for her. But after lunch she had made her tea and went out. He had stayed indoors, his own book open in his lap and the radio Ellen had packed tuned to the local news. There would be a New Year's smorgasbord at the East Sound Community Center, fireworks following; precipitation expected over the holiday. Loren imagined old Swedes in rain slickers, their sparklers too damp to light, and he smiled. He wasn't certain how people stood to live here, locked in, the woolen smother of the sea air and the close lapping of the water on all sides, as if the world had shrunk. The island was too removed, too cut off from the life going on in the cities across the Sound. The only way off the island was the ferry, and that seemed oppressive, too; even if one wanted to go, the leaving had to be planned, timed according to the ferry schedule. Most year-round residents were retirees, the woman at the resort office had told Ellen. Retirees had the money to afford island property, and they didn't need to worry about getting off the island very often. Still, retirement here seemed like a terrible idea to Loren—a kind of self-imposed confinement.

Outside the window, he saw that Ellen was now leaning over the railing, carrying on a conversation with the couple as if they were long-lost friends. They looked young. They didn't seem to have suitcases, just backpacking packs, which they carried on their backs as if they'd be hiking down the beach to pitch camp instead of just stepping into the cabin next door. The woman hugged two bed pillows against her rather ample chest. She smiled and nodded as Ellen spoke, and then the conversation ended, and Ellen waved and came back inside, a rush of chill air gusting in behind her. Her face was pink, and she pulled off her hat, ruffled her hair so that it lay mussed about her head.

"They're nice," she said. And then, lower, as if she were gossiping, scandalized: "They're so young!" She had brought in her tea and dumped it into the sink, rinsed the cup and filled the kettle to boil more water. "I've invited them for dinner tomorrow night," she said. "They can't spend New Year's Eve alone. They have no one out here."

Loren closed his book. "That's the point, isn't it?" he said. "The point of the holiday on the island is that you have no one."

"We'll have them over," she said. "New Year's Eve is meant to be a party." She tugged at the sleeves of her sweater, slid free of it, and hung it over the back of the chair. The turtleneck she wore underneath fit close against her thin chest. *She's a spindle, isn't she?* a doctor had commented to Loren once, and Loren had thought of his wife's sewing machine, the punctured movement of the needle, the fine metal bones of the machine, and the frantic motion of the bobbin spinning as she sewed.

Ellen bustled about in the kitchen for a few moments while she waited for the kettle to whistle, washing their lunch plates and stacking them away, wiping down the countertops. The news program Loren had been listening to ended, and the station hummed for a few seconds with static silence before a piano concerto began. This is how things were at home: the two of them sharing the space of an afternoon without filling it. Hours might pass before he looked up from his book and spoke to her, before she needed him for something—a word for her crossword puzzle, a hand with setting the dinner table or opening the wine—but Loren was aware of her presence in an abstract way, and so he did not feel alone. Before she was sick, this is how things were.

"I suppose it will be fine," Loren said. "If they come to dinner."

"We'll clam-dig," Ellen said. "You can barbecue."

On the stove, the kettle whistled, and she turned her back to him to pour her tea.

By evening, clouds swelled in the sky, thick and heavy as gray knitted blankets. They muffled any moonlight there might have been, and cast only their own damp half-light on the water and the beach. Ellen went out to walk once more before bed, anyway. She put a mittened hand on Loren's shoulder, kissed his cheek as she left.

Loren gave her a few moments and then put on his coat, moved outside to sit on the porch and keep an eye on her. She had taken a flashlight, and its halo bobbed in the distance with her movement, the light stretching into a thin beam when she raised her hand to illuminate the sand ahead. Above her, the clouds shifted almost imperceptibly with the bit of wind coming off the Sound. They took on the strange gray-green cast of the water, like the color of an old bruise, as the tide began to rise for the night, the waves narrowing the beach to just a strip of sand, disappearing the piece of driftwood Ellen had sat on during her earlier walk.

Loren put his feet up on the porch railing, resting the metal frame of his chair against the cabin wall, then teetered when he shifted his weight, so that his body flinched in reflexive fear. He remembered sitting this way as a child—the fun of it, trying to balance—but he felt precarious and foolish rocking in his chair now, so he put his feet down again, sat stiff-legged, straight and safe, his arms folded across his chest.

"You wouldn't have fallen." It was the woman from next door, though for an instant Loren was confused, thought her voice Ellen's. She stood in the driveway between the two cabins, her truck pulled into the space now and the tailgate open. It was dark, and he couldn't see her face. "You looked steady there to me."

"Oh," Loren said, embarrassed. "I didn't know I had an audience." He could see his breath, and then, when he looked more closely into the thick darkness, he could see hers as well, a slim exhale, a fine blue cloud where her mouth must have been.

Behind her, the curtains were drawn in her cabin, but the lights were on. He wondered if her cabin was a replica of Ellen's and his inside, or if there were differences—a smaller kitchen, a bigger bathtub, a softer bed. He looked down the beach and searched for Ellen's light.

The woman slammed the truck's tailgate shut and moved closer, put her mittened hands on Loren's porch railing, so that he stood and stuffed his own hands into his coat pockets, sniffed in a breath of the cold air and looked down at her.

"You think the mini-mart is still open at this hour?" she asked.

"They close," Loren said. "They close at seven." He moved to pull the cuff of his coat up over his wrist, squinted to see his watch face. "It must be past eight now."

"I've forgotten firewood," she said. Ellen had been right: She was young. Not even thirty yet—a girl, really—and she had her blonde hair in two braids over her shoulders, her ski cap pulled down over her ears, so that it was difficult to tell her age exactly, so that she looked younger still than she likely was.

"You could collect driftwood," Loren said, and the girl nodded, turned back to her truck. "I didn't really mean that," Loren said then. "I was joking. It was supposed to be a joke. We have wood inside."

He went into the cabin, and bent and sorted through the wood he'd stacked, picking out the heavier pieces, the driest and best ones, setting aside an armload. They should have thought ahead, those kids; he'd have to buy more himself tomorrow now. He found twine in a kitchen drawer and got down on his knees to bundle the wood.

The girl had come in behind him and stood on the rug near the door for a moment, then crossed the room toward him. He could see her face clearly with the light inside and recognized what he had noticed about her through the window earlier in the day. She was fairer and taller than Ellen, her figure heavier set and solid inside her winter jacket and her jeans; and she moved her body in the way a girl athlete might—a swimmer or a skier. As if everything she did was one continuous motion. In a dress she would be pretty.

"I appreciate it," the girl said. "We brought sleeping bags to put on the bed, but we might have frozen."

"It's fine," Loren told her. He stood, lifted the wood, and she leaned close to him, taking one bundle under each arm, her braids swinging out and brushing the chest of his coat.

"No, we'll bring you some wood tomorrow. We'll go up to the store in the morning."

Loren nodded, put his hands back into his pockets. "Fine," he said. "Fine. You can just leave it on the porch. No rush."

He held the door open for her and watched her step down the stoop and cross the strip of sand between the two cabins. He thought the man she was with might step out of their cabin to say thank you, but when the girl reached the door, she opened it herself and went in. The lights stayed on behind her windows another few moments and then shut off.

Inside his own cabin, Loren added the last of the wood to his fire, then went into the bathroom and brushed his teeth. Ellen had hung her bathrobe on the hook near the tub, and when he opened the mirrored medicine chest above the sink, he saw that she had lined up her cosmetics on the narrow glass shelves inside: plastic cases holding squares of powder in pink, fleshy tones; a metal tube of lipstick; a silver compact pressed with a fleur-de-lis pattern that he took out, and held in his palm, and opened and shut. He could remember her taking the compact out of her purse early on—when he first knew her—eyeing herself at close range in the small mirror. Even then she had been older than the girl.

"What are you doing in here? Admiring yourself?" Ellen had finished her walk, and she knocked as she opened the bathroom door, came in on him, her sweater still on and her hands cold at his neck when she touched him.

"Your friends were here," he said. "They didn't think about wood when they packed those backpacks." He closed the compact and returned it to the shelf.

"They're young," Ellen said. "I'm sure they were focused on other ways of staying warm." She smiled, sat on the ledge of the tub and turned on the faucet, then bent to untie and remove her shoes, her socks.

In the slant reflection of the medicine chest mirror, Loren could see his wife's body. He hadn't often seen her without her clothes since she fell sick, and seeing her now that she was well again shocked him. Not because she was thinner or more angular, her back beginning to round the way older women's did—though these things were all true. It was simply the foreignness of her naked that surprised him, like seeing a stranger nude. They both felt this, and just as he lowered his eyes, she turned her back to him before taking her clothes and folding them into a stack on the toilet's tank. She kept her face turned away from him when she dipped her hand into the bathwater to check the temperature before climbing in.

"You've become so grouchy in your old age," Ellen said to him. "Even you must have been young once, too."

She lay still beneath the water for a moment, a washcloth soaked and spread to cover her chest, her eyes closed, then sat up and began to wash her arms, her legs. When she was at her weakest, he'd worried he would have to do this for her—bathe her. He'd been racked with guilt when he admitted it to himself, but the truth was that he didn't want to see her body then, and her need. He didn't want to ruin her for himself.

Steam clouded the mirror, and the room smelled heavily of Ellen's astringent soap and of the cedar paneling that ribbed the walls.

"I'll keep the bedside light on," Loren said, and he shut the medicine chest, and turned to leave the room.

"You were probably just as you are now when you were young," Ellen went on, dunking for an instant beneath the water to rinse the soap from her skin. She set her bar of soap on the tub's ledge, pulled the plug at her feet so that the drain sputtered and gulped for air, and climbed out of the bath reaching for her robe. "I probably wouldn't have married you then. Picture that." She walked ahead of him out of the bathroom, her feet still wet and leaving prints on the wood floor. "Picture meeting me at thirty and being dumped instead of married." She laughed and opened the closet door in the bedroom, stood behind it pulling on her pajamas.

In bed later, Loren lay on his side, away from the light of her reading lamp, listening as she turned the pages of her book. The wind had picked up outside, and there was the sound of rain on the roof of the cabin—not a real rain, but rain pulled up from the sea as the wind passed over it. He listened for the gust against the glass of the bedroom windows, and then the shudder of rain hitting the thin shingles of the roof, and then the quiet again. The sound of waves. The sound of breeze in the sea grass, mimicking the waves.

Across the strip of sand, in the next cabin, he imagined the young couple lying beneath their opened sleeping bags. He could see the slope of the girl's shoulders in the dark bedroom, the blond length of her hair unbraided and splayed like an open fan across her pillow, the boy's hands trembling across the bare plane of her abdomen. Loren's own stomach tightened. He closed his eyes and saw the girl with her hair the color of prairie grass—that's what it reminded him of, grass on an open prairie—her runner's legs sprawled across that wide other bed. He lay as still as he could envisioning this.

In the twenty-five years of his marriage to Ellen, Loren had never been unfaithful, but Ellen had. He didn't dwell on it often anymore, though when she was sick there were moments when he imagined what his life might have been if he had left her then, if he had not been so afraid to let her go. No one would have blamed him for going then.

The man Ellen had been with was an attorney at the office where she worked as a paralegal. Loren had seen him only once, at an office picnic that summer—the summer of their first wedding anniversary and of Ellen's indiscretion. Later, once Ellen had confessed and he had forgiven her, Loren considered his memory of the other man. The man had the sort of broad shoulders Loren supposed women liked, and Loren could see that he probably looked well holding Ellen, that they would appear suited to each other in a way that Loren and Ellen were not. There are some people, Loren had always reasoned, who are just a bit more ebullient, more charming, more athletic than everyone else. Ellen was among this group; so was the man.

Later, Ellen told him that she had started up with the man because of tennis. Because the man invited her to play one evening after work—because they'd become a sort of team in the minds of their coworkers—an unbeatable team, she said. "We were unbeatable at doubles."

Loren could picture Ellen's body as it had been then beside the man's on a tennis court—her white skirt just revealing her thighs, her calves already tensed in anticipation of the other man's next move.

Of course, Loren had not left her, and he had felt relieved that she did not leave him. He tried to but could not picture a life without her, on his own, and so he forgave her and became in Ellen's mind and everyone else's the best kind of husband.

There were times now, though, when he did consider the alternative life he might have lived if he had gone. There was a kind of sorry revenge in envisioning a life free of her, of her illness, of the burden he had taken on in becoming her redeemer. After her affair, she believed Loren a better person than her; she believed she needed him, rather than the other way around.

When she got sick, there were times when Loren imagined himself abandoning her, abandoning his earlier decision to forgive. *It's not my problem*, he imagined himself saying to her. He let his mind roll the words around like small stones in a closed hand.

The following day, New Year's Eve, Ellen sent him out to dig for razor clams during the mid-morning low tide. "Go," she said, shooing him out of the cabin. "Go on before the water's up again." She had been up to the resort's office and had brought back for him a metal pail and a wooden-handled trench shovel that he carried over his shoulder like a ski as he walked down the beach toward the dark legs of the pier. The pier extended from the resort office's front walk and ran a hundred feet or so out into the water. During a high tide, the water would lap just a few inches below its deck, but the pilings were visible now, still wet and coated in a shiny black gloss of creosote, graffitied with strands of seaweed and gray barnacle colonies that emitted a stiff, salty odor. Loren stopped beneath them and set down his pail, dug his shovel into the sand.

"You can't see the clams," Ellen told him when he left the cabin. "You have to be quiet and still and wait for them to spit." She had read a pamphlet at the office, and demonstrated for him the way he should step around the little pits the clams made in the sand, to encourage their spitting. They could bury themselves more quickly than he would be able to shovel, she warned, and he should be careful about cracking their shells with the blade as he dug; they would never open on the barbecue if he broke their shells.

Loren bent and looked for the divots that indicated clams. He tapped his foot around in the soft sand, watching the way his footsteps left welts, putting his weight down hard when he found a half-shell left by a seagull, and listening for the satisfying sound of its break. Near one of the pilings, fishermen had dropped the waste of their catch for the gulls to feed on. Loren looked away from the greenish mound of innards, nauseated, but toed the fine bones of a spine, a frail corset that had somehow held the fish's body intact.

Eventually, he gave up, lugged the pail and the shovel back up to the office, and started again for the cabin. He would take the car to the market, buy clams somebody else had already dug and cleaned.

The girl was on her porch as he walked down the beach, and she shouted to him as he passed her. "I'm headed out to get that wood for you," she said. She stooped to tie the laces on her hiking boots, smiled at him. Her hair hung down her back and over her shoulders, loose.

"Don't worry about it," Loren said. "I have to pick a few things up myself now. I'll just get it."

The girl stood and tugged down the waist of her jacket. "I'll come with you, then, if that's all right. Save a little gas." She followed him around the side of his cabin to where the car was parked and let herself in on Ellen's side, where she sat, mittened hands between her knees, waiting for him.

He stood with his hand on the driver's-side door and looked to the cabin, wondered if he should go inside and tell Ellen the girl was coming along—just for propriety's sake, not because Ellen would care.

"Are we ready?" the girl said inside the car, though, and so Loren got in beside her and shut the door, backed out slowly over the sand.

It was not a long drive into town, but it seemed longer in the car with her, the heater on and blowing, and the radio tuned to the local station again, a male voice reading aloud the day's tide chart. The roadway was wet, and the wind the night before had knocked branches from the alders and the cedars that Loren had to swerve to avoid.

"You didn't need to worry about the wood," Loren said.

"No, it's fine. I haven't been into town yet, anyway. We came the other direction from the ferry, a back route. I should get something to bring to your dinner tonight, too." She kept her face turned toward the window as they passed the slouching houses of the island's year-round residents. The roofs were all deep beneath browning pine needles and wet leaves, and strands of Christmas lights that had been blown down hung lank from gutters and front-yard cedar trees. Loren thought he should have told Ellen he was leaving with the girl. It felt dishonest driving with her beside him now, and he turned to look at her once when he shifted, then again as they turned a slight corner in the road. "Did I miss your name?" he asked her. He needed something to say. "I have a problem with names. With remembering them. Or, rather, with forgetting them, I suppose." He was adolescent in his bumbling. "You probably told me last night, and I've forgotten already."

"No." The girl smiled. "It's Lucia."

"Lucia," he repeated. The name stuck in his mouth. His tongue thickened with the hushing sound of the second syllable.

"Yes. Lucia."

"I've heard of those girls," he said. "The Lucia girls in Scandinavia. Norway or Sweden, I can't remember now. They bring doughnuts on Christmas morning, or something like that." He'd seen pictures of the girls—young and dressed in white gowns with red sashes. They wore candles on their heads in wreaths.

"They say it differently," she told him. "Lu-see-ah."

"Oh, right," he said. "And you're Lu-sha. Lu-sha," he said again, overemphasizing its two syllables as if they were separate words. He smiled at her.

The girl nodded and shifted away from him then to look out the window, and Loren turned up the radio to keep himself from saying anything more.

He could smell the scent of her shampoo, a scent like leaves or summer grass that might have been perfume or just the scent of her skin, and he rolled down the driver's-side window a crack, felt the chill stream of air rush in near his face.

At the market, Loren bought clams from the seafood counter and then stood at the front of the store, waiting for her. He rummaged in the bags and then set them at his feet, stood with his hands in his pockets and then folded his arms across his chest. The stance just made him look impatient, though—or cross—and so he bent down again and picked up the bags and stood holding them to his chest.

"Sorry," Lucia said when she finished her shopping. "That took a while." She had bought three stacks of wood for him that he piled into the trunk while she settled herself again up front. Even once he had taken his seat beside her and began to drive, Loren could smell the raw pine, the sap that sweated from the wood where the bark had been stripped. "The clerk said you looked bored," she said, and then she laughed. "It was funny. She actually said, 'Your husband looks bored.'"

"Really," Loren said. He couldn't look at her. "That is funny."

On the radio, two men discussed the best way to prepare a fish while still out on the water, whether it was better to just open it and gut it, or to fillet it out there, too. Loren thought about the fish he had seen on the beach earlier, the threads of intestine and the needle-thin bones. He tasted bile at the back of his tongue and swallowed. "I couldn't do that," he said, nodding toward the radio. "Gut them. I couldn't fish."

"That's too bad," the girl said. "I guess you'd miss a good dinner." She smiled until Loren smiled, too.

Ahead of him, through his windshield, the water came into view, the sky heavy-bellied with dusk already and the water white-capped with wind.

Beside him, the girl leaned her head against the window and closed her eyes. If she was sleeping, maybe he could touch her hair, just to feel the blunt edge of its ends against his fingers. But he didn't move.

At the beach again, he let her out in front of her cabin.

"Thanks for the ride," she said, leaning down to look at him through the still-open door. Her blond braid dangled over her shoulder. "I'm looking forward to dinner tonight."

"Oh, sure," said Loren. He lifted his hand in a half-wave. "No problem."

He sat in the idling car and watched her cross the bank of sand toward the cabin steps. At the door she turned. "You don't have to wait," she hollered to him. "If I get locked out, I'll just come next door." She had a wide grin, and shook her head at him and laughed.

"Oh, sure," Loren said again, nodding to himself. His manners were ridiculous out here. "Of course not." He waved once more, then pulled forward into the driveway.

Ellen took a bath before the neighbors arrived, combed her short hair behind her ears so that her face seemed more revealed, her eyes bright and sharp blue-gray as fieldstones. She dressed in wool pants and a bulky red sweater, then shuffled across the wood floor in her heavy socks to the kitchen to begin dinner. When they knocked, she spun away from the stove, the spoon still in her hand, and beamed at Loren. "It's them," she whispered. "Get the door."

They both wore sweaters and jeans, and the young man—who was tall and gangly and stubble-faced—had on a fleece cap with flaps that hung down over his ears. He carried a six-pack of beer in one hand and kept his other arm close around the girl's waist. She had a loaf of garlic bread in a foil wrapper cradled in her arms and broke away from the young man to hold it out to Loren, to lean forward and put her cold cheek against his in greeting. "Thanks again for the ride today," she said.

"Did he take you with him?" Ellen said from the stove. She lifted her hand to wave to the young couple, smiled. "You didn't tell me that, Loren. He didn't tell me," she said to the girl. "Did you go along, too?" she asked the young man, and when he shook his head, she smiled, turned back to stir her potatoes, said Loren was good about sparing her errands.

The cabin was warm and felt smaller with four people inside instead of just two, and Loren went to the front window and opened it slightly. He felt strangely possessive of the place, and therefore ashamed of it—as if he ought to be able to provide better accommodations than the soft, slumping couch, the cheap table Ellen had set with the mismatched plates and silverware from the cabin cabinets. At the narrow kitchen counter, Loren opened a bottle of wine, poured it into four jelly glasses, and excused himself to check on the clams.

The hibachi they'd borrowed from the resort sat on the porch, putting out an aura of heat, and Loren opened his hands over it, moved the joints of his fingers to warm them. He could hear the conversation inside through the open window, Ellen going on about another New Year's Eve, a party they'd attended, too much champagne. The girl laughed, and then Ellen laughed, and for a moment Loren could not tell whose voice was whose. He opened the lid on the hibachi, poked at the closed lips of the clamshells with the fork he'd brought out from the kitchen.

He remembered that New Year's. They were a few years married, and the party was one of those thrown by a city—a gala, the city called it—a ticketed event he considered far too expensive, but Ellen wanted to go. They'd dressed up—he wore a tuxedo with the new cuff links Ellen had given him for Christmas, a red wool scarf that he put around his neck because she said it made him look festive and jolly. "Saint Nick," she said, and pinched his cheek. "Saint Nick of the modern age." She wore her hair long then, and it was darker, though already graying, and she pinned it up so that all evening he noticed her shoulders—bare and slim—the frame of her collarbones and the pearls suspended just below her earlobes.

But they had drunk too much, and there was a taxi ride home, a bill the next day from the towing service that had taken care of their car, a headache Loren could still feel if he thought about it.

On the other side of the cabin window he could hear Ellen remembering that night aloud for the young couple.

Loren stood on the porch, finishing his wine. The sun had set behind the clouds, and the gray sky had deepened to dusk and now to darkness. Far out, a cruiser strung with Christmas lights bobbed in the water, and the tide that had receded again made its measured sound.

"I've been sent to ask you about the clams," the girl said, stepping out onto the porch in her stockinged feet and closing the door behind her. She held a beer and sipped from it, her face still ruddy with the indoor heat. "Your wife is great," she said. "She has Adam cooking with her." The girl gestured toward the window, and Loren leaned to see inside, where the young man stood at the stove with Ellen.

The young man and Lucia were an ill-matched couple, and he seemed the sort who must have felt startled, dumbfounded by his own luck at attracting the girl. Loren had noticed the way he'd kept his arm around her earlier, when they first came in. It was the way all young men held their girlfriends—a grip too eager, too possessive.

The girl sat down in the lawn chair and crossed one leg over the other, sat drinking her beer.

"You don't like wine?" Loren asked.

"No," she said, "what you poured was good. I just thought I'd try this, too. It's local." She held the bottle out to him, and he hesitated but took it. The lip of the bottle was still wet when he sipped from it.

"It's good," he said, though it was bitter and stung at the back of his throat so that he had to swallow quickly. He passed the bottle back to her, wiped his hand across his mouth.

She was quiet awhile, looking out at the boat, Loren thought, the blur of the lights on its deck in the distance the only bright thing in sight. He imagined the people on the boat drinking their champagne, eating their dinner, ready to pull anchor in the morning, unweighted and off to somewhere unfamiliar and new. He thought about the girl with her pack on her back the day before. The way he saw her life, she was as unattached as that boat—no job he had heard of and not married to the awkward man inside the cabin. Had he met her a few months earlier—in his regular life at home—Loren might have thought her irresponsible, a belated adolescent, but out here her ease was desirable. He imagined again her head on a pillow, her hair bright and free of its braid.

He opened the lid on the hibachi and peered in at the wide-open mouths of the clams, the pink tongues of meat on each shell. "They're done," he said.

The girl stood up and picked out a clam, held it by the edge of its shell. "I have to admit," she said, "I don't know how to eat these things. I've had them in chowder, but never this way." She made a face. "I'm not sure I want one."

Loren chose his own clam and used the fork to free the meat from the shell. The clam was buttered, and his mouth watered around the meat before he swallowed. He moved toward the girl then and took the clam she held, slid the meat onto his fork, and offered it to her. The hard edge of her front teeth hit the metal of his fork as she took her bite.

The girl looked away from him. She covered her mouth with her hand and chewed behind her fingers.

On the other side of the window, Ellen and the young man sat across the table from each other with their drinks, and they laughed now over some joke.

The girl stepped away from Loren. "I think I should go," she said. She turned and went inside, and in a moment he saw her take the chair beside her boyfriend, saw her reach for his hand.

* * *

They ate in the heat of the cabin, all of the windows open a crack now and the glass beaded with the sweat of condensation. Ellen served a salmon, baked in garlic and butter and rosemary; potatoes still in their red skins; salad and bread and red and white wine that the four of them drank slowly through the evening. Ellen hadn't drunk much since she'd been sick—because of the drugs, and because of the way everything tasted sharp and coppered, she said, even good wine like a mouthful of pennies. But she drank a glass over the New Year's dinner she'd prepared, and her face pinked, and her eyes became wetter, and she reached to touch Loren's hand when the young man explained how he'd met Lucia—on a bus, he said, on his way to work at a bookstore in Portland, where they both lived.

"We met because of my clumsiness," Ellen said. "I stepped off a curb wrong at a crosswalk. I turned my ankle."

"You caught her," the girl said to Loren, smiling. She was drinking wine with dinner, and she lifted her jelly glass again, holding it out for the young man to refill.

"No," Loren said. "I just helped her up."

Ellen looked at him. "I was already on my feet," she said. "But he took my elbow. It was unnecessary chivalry." She laughed. "It's his favorite part of the story—the part where he becomes the hero." She slapped at Loren's hand and leaned to kiss his cheek.

"I would've looked like an ass if I hadn't stopped to help you," Loren said. His head felt loose, his thoughts sloppy. He felt his wife lift her hand from his, her lips grazing his cheek. Across the table, the girl's hair shone in the light of the room, and he thought of the candies he'd loved as a child—coins wrapped in gold foil, the smooth feel of the foil against his thumb before he unfolded it, peeled it away from around the chocolate.

"Don't say it that way, Loren," Ellen said. "It was kind. That was all either of us thought then—that you were being kind."

No one spoke.

The girl finished her wine, and Loren folded his napkin in his lap and listened to the tidal sound of blood rushing behind his eardrums.

"It is too warm in here," Ellen said then, finally, and she stood and began to clear the table. They should go out, she said. She wanted to walk.

Out on the beach, the darkness had settled, and the air was thin and cool skimming in off the water. The clouds the weatherman had predicted on the radio had not rolled in, and there were a few stars—high and distant—and a sliver of moon over the low tide and the wide slick of black sand.

Ellen and the young man started out for the pier as Loren sat on the porch stoop to retie his shoelaces. The girl sat next to him. "You need a minute?" Ellen called, and turned, walking backward so that she could face them. "I'll see you there, Loren," she said. When she turned away again, her stride matching the young man's, she lit her flashlight, and the beam jostled and bounced on the sand before her.

"She's not so independent at home," Loren said to the girl. He bent over his left shoe, and his breath came out in puffs in the chill air. "She hasn't been for a long time."

The girl didn't wear mittens, but tucked her hands into the cuffs of her sweater like a child. "It's good you brought her, then," she said. "They say the sea air is healthy. It was good of you to bring her."

"Ellen wanted to come," Loren said. "My wife. It was her idea. She says what you say: It's better here."

The girl smiled. "You must agree," she said. "She told me earlier—when you went out to bake those clams—that you watch her. That you stand out here on the porch when she walks. She said you like that you can keep an eye on her here. 'I'm in sight here,' she said." The girl paused.

"It's nice to hope that's still ahead of me," she said then. She turned to Loren, looked at him. "You know what I mean? Romance."

Loren sat still. He thought of what Ellen had said during dinner—that it had been chivalry when he took her arm that day they met. That he had done the kind thing in helping her.

It wasn't kindness, though, he remembered, because he'd been glad that she had tripped. He'd walked away from her that afternoon, her phone number in his pocket, feeling struck by the certain lift of chance. The grace of his own good luck.

Now, on the beach, Loren squinted in the direction of the pier until he found the frail beam of the flashlight darting from here to there in the darkness. He could just make out the shape of the young man's figure, and beside him, Ellen. She had her feet in the water. She stood at the very edge of the moving tide.

"I'm going to catch up with them," the girl said. She stood from the stoop and started down the beach, and in a few moments, Loren got up as well and walked at a distance from her, toward the narrow beam of Ellen's flashlight, the sound of laughter beneath the spidery legs of the pier.

"I read," Ellen was saying when he arrived, "that some people burn things to celebrate." She had pulled her hat down over her ears again, buttoned her sweater to the neck. She took Loren's arm when he moved to stand beside her.

"Prayers," the young man agreed. "I've heard of cultures writing down and burning prayers. The smoke is like an offering."

"No, no. I was thinking something that would float on the water and only eventually burn out," Ellen said. "Floating candles, maybe. It's meant to burn off the old year. To bring light into the new one."

The girl laughed. "I'm thinking of Viking burials now," she said. "Isn't that a pleasant image to start the year?"

"I guess it doesn't really matter what you burn," Ellen said. "I'm picturing it, though: four flames on the water." She raised the beam on the flashlight so that it illuminated a strip of sand and sea. The water nearest the shore moved with the slow current of low tide, the thin lip of one wave disappearing into the next, and farther out, past the shore, a sea black and placid and extending, vast and dark beyond the length of the beam.

Loren squinted. He wanted to see what Ellen was seeing. He couldn't even really see the water—where it began and ended, or the shape of the waves coming toward him. He could only see the boat he had spotted earlier, farther out now, just the pinpoints of the holiday lights on its deck, floating and suspended but distinct in the dark mess of water and sky, bound by fragile cords to the invisible boat.

FAMILIAL KINDNESS

ALMA WAS SWEEPING THE STOOP when Charlie's car appeared at the end of the road. Though she recognized her brother-in-law right away, she did not put down her broom or walk out to the drive to wave him in. He was not expected. She had sent him an invitation to the wedding, and she supposed he felt obliged, but the invitation had been a formality—a familial kindness—and in truth she had not actually wished to see him at all.

In the drive, he stopped his car and looked at her through the glass of the windshield a moment before getting out, then stood at a distance instead of walking toward her and raised a hand in greeting. "Alma," he said. "It's Charlie Dunne."

Alma nodded. "You can come in once I finish this," she said. "You walk through this sand, and it'll be all over my carpets in a minute." She whisked the broom across the cement in short strokes. She'd spent her life sweeping sand from this house, it seemed. Sand that blew up from the beach and banked against the house in great drifts; sand that lay like a fine layer of dust along the window ledges and in the corners of the rooms inside. If she had collected all of the sand she had swept from this house since her childhood, Alma would have had buckets full. She let out a breath and then leaned the broom against the stoop's railing beside the front door and invited Charlie in. "I didn't know you'd be coming," she said. "I can make coffee, though. You drink coffee, don't you?"

Charlie followed her inside and trudged down the hallway behind her, his footsteps loud on the floorboards. She hadn't had a man in the house—no man other than Lovisa's James—since her father had passed, though, and she wondered if it was Charlie who had heavy feet, or she who was sensitive now to a man's weight on the floor, a man's presence in her kitchen as she moved toward the sink to fill the coffeepot with water.

"You'll barely recognize Lovisa," she said. "I sent Sara all her school photos—maybe you saw—but she's been out a full year now, and you wouldn't know her to meet her on the street." Alma turned, set the pot on to percolate, and gestured to the table, where Charlie pulled out a chair and sat.

"I saw the photos," he said. "She's a good-looking girl. She looks a little like Sara."

"You think so?" Alma said. "I don't see that."

Charlie sat with his hands opened, palms down, on the tabletop, the fingers splayed wide apart. He no longer wore his wedding band, though there was a groove where it had been all those years—the finger thinner there, and the skin pale and still polished by the rub of the metal. He had sent Alma her sister's ring when Sara died. Odd, Alma thought at the time, though she'd put it on a chain that she wore around her neck, beneath her clothes.

The kitchen table was cluttered, and Charlie had needed to push her sewing kit aside, nudge the Singer toward the wall to clear a space for himself. She might have tidied the place if she'd known he was coming, but as it was, a week from the wedding and Lovisa's dress still just pattern pieces and a bolt of white satin, she didn't apologize. The table was crowded with boxes .of ribbon and bunches of blue fabricated flowers on plastic stems, three bags of birdseed Lovisa wanted bundled and passed out as favors; and in the other room, the armless, naked form on which the dress would be fitted stood like the Venus de Milo next to the couch. Upstairs, Alma was certain Lovisa had not cleaned the bathroom in at least two weeks. There were likely long hairs clinging to the sides of the sink, Lovisa's razor on the tub ledge, damp towels left in piles on the tiled floor. Alma would have to get up there before Charlie could settle his things.

Alma faced her brother-in-law as she waited at the counter for the coffee. "I guess you and Sara kept a nice house for yourselves," she said. "Her letters always mentioned the lawn."

"She liked the place," Charlie said. "She did it up with curtains and new carpeting, and she put a gazebo out back—one of those you buy already made." He worked the grain of the table with his finger-nails. "We did have a big lawn," he said, and looked to Alma. "Sod, not seed. Sara was tired of a yard full of sand."

"Sara was homesick," Alma said. "Maybe you couldn't see."

"All respect," Charlie said, "but I don't think you knew her well enough to say." He shifted in his chair, and the wooden legs squeaked against the wooden floor.

On the counter, the coffeepot gurgled to full, and Alma turned and reached to open the cupboard for mugs, the tiny pitcher meant for cream.

Alma had not seen Charlie since the day of his own wedding thirty years before. He and Sara had been married at the house in a cere-mony intended for the beach, but brought inside when the sky clouded over and a heavy rain began. Sara's dress had gotten wet, the satin streaked and the puffs of the lace sleeves soaked flat against her arms, and though Alma had taken her up to the bathroom to fix her makeup and blow-dry the dress, she had not been entirely sorry to see the day ruined. Later, after the ceremony and the cake, Charlie escorted her sister out to the brown station wagon that sat waiting in the drive, its windows snowed in shaving cream and its bumper burdened with old shoes on fishing line, and drove Sara to the Greyhound station, where they caught a bus for Spokane and then a train bound for Chicago. Within a month, they'd bought the house in Indiana, in Charlie's hometown, and had never come back west.

In the meantime, Alma had stayed on this beach along the coast of the Washington peninsula. She took over the house when her parents passed—first her mother fifteen years ago of the same cancer that later ended Sara's life, and then her father the following year, of pneumonia. Alma had raised her daughter alone, never marrying the dull boyfriend who'd fathered her. And now Lovisa would be leaving, too, after the wedding on Saturday—getting on the Greyhound just as Sara had done, but this time taking the bus north, to Bellingham, and then boarding the ferry to Alaska with her new husband, moving to what might as well have been another continent.

When Alma tried to imagine Alaska, she could see only weather—weather without landscape—clouds vast and gray and rolling like the bodies of whales as the wind turned them. Snow that blotted out everything. Ice like great sheets of white wedding satin. She tried to picture Lovisa up there, standing on a plot of grass or sitting comfortably on a kitchen chair inside the squat house James owned in Kenai and had described to them. But when she did this, Lovisa's face became indistinct, and Alma had to stop her daydream and reassure herself that it would be impossible for her to ever forget her own daughter's features.

In the years since Sara had left, Alma had written her often. Sara only rarely replied, but Alma went on, reliably writing one letter a week, always by hand, because it seemed more personal than typing them out and so spoke to the kind of time and attention she thought a sister deserved. She wrote about the daily things mostly, because she wasn't certain what else one said in a letter, and she always invited her sister home.

OCTOBER 3, 1982

The weather remains gloomy. Rain through the night and all day. Lovisa is learning the state capitals at school—Olympia, Montpelier, Tallahassee, etc.—and scored high marks on her math test. We're expecting warmer temperatures after this week, and a nice June if you want to come out for a visit.

MAY 19, 1990

Saturday was busy with laundry and the usual. The fish at the market in town have gone down in quality lately—frozen and shipped in, rather than off our own boats. But you have to buy what they sell, don't you? Lovisa will work after school gets out next month. The J.C. Penney hires two high school girls a year. You should take the train out. I know you'd be happy to come and rest awhile—let me take care of things while you just vacation.

DECEMBER 8, 1994

Lovisa will marry this summer. She wants to wear your dress—she's seen the photos. You don't have to send it—she's tall anyway. I'll find the old pattern and make it to her size. She'd like you to come for the week.

This last letter had gone without a response, though. By the time it left Alma's mailbox and crossed the mountains, the wide middle of the country, and the blue dotted line that ran like a fence around Indiana, Sara was gone.

Alma waited two weeks, and then finally a return letter did arrive, the envelope written out in Charlie's blocky hand, and inside a copy of the death announcement cut from the local paper, Sara's ring in a baggie, and a short note that read only:

Alma: She'd been undone a long time. Her will requested cremation, and I didn't hold a service. I thought you'd appreciate the ring. ~ Charlie Dunne

Alma sat at the kitchen table with the clipping and the letter and the baggie placed in front of her. She looked at them, moved them around, rearranging their order on the tabletop, as if they were jigsaw pieces, fragments of an image that would form a full picture if set right. She took the ring from the baggie and tried it on her ring finger first, then her little finger, then she got up and climbed the stairs to her bedroom, fumbled through the mess of costume jewelry in the pretty wooden box that had been her mother's until she found a gold chain sturdy enough to trust. In front of the dressing mirror, Alma unfastened the top two buttons of her blouse, reached up, and clasped the chain around her neck. The ring hung heavy just below the dip between her collarbones. It rested there against her chest, and even after she buttoned her blouse again and descended the stairs, folded the letter and the clipping in the envelope, put them away and went to the sink to start washing potatoes for supper, she could feel the ring against her skin—the cool weight of the metal, the rough edges of the prongs that grasped her sister's diamond like tiny, greedy hands.

She drove into town the next day and bought Charlie a condolence card at the drugstore—a picture of a blue sky, vast and vacant and sunny, above a glassy plane of water on which a single boat floated, its sail puffed taut with courage. Inside, the card read, *With Deepest Sympathy,* and beneath the lettering Alma signed her name and Lovisa's before dropping the card into the postbox on the sidewalk outside the store.

When Lovisa still hadn't arrived home by late evening, Alma and Charlie ate dinner without her, and then Charlie volunteered to take care of the dishes while Alma climbed the stairs to tidy the bathroom and opened the windows in the guest bedroom for him—the bedroom that had once been Sara's. The room didn't see many visitors, and when Alma opened the door, it smelled like an old closet, the sheets on the bed stale with the scent of mildew that grew too easily in the salty humidity of the sea air. She stripped the bed and was opening the trunk at the footboard to find new sheets when Charlie entered the room and stood at the doorway, his suitcase in hand.

"I thought I'd unpack the car," he said, and jostled the case. It was a hard-shelled Samsonite with the old kind of metal clasps. There would be a satin pocket inside, for keeping one's underthings tucked away, and a hidden pocket for jewelry.

Alma had a suitcase just the same in the attic somewhere, and had once—just after Lovisa's birth—taken it out and packed it, considered buying a ticket to Chicago and calling her sister from a bus station there. She'd wondered what it would be like to disappear. She'd imagined the relief of vanishing as she packed her heavy winter coat and the three dresses she had that still fit, a pair of knitted tights she thought would be useful in the cold Midwestern December. It would be as if she'd slipped her skin, evaporated, the way she had seen storm clouds rise off the water on the horizon before sliding, a moment later, back into the gray line of the ocean. It would be release.

Of course, she hadn't gone. There was the baby to consider, and her parents—though they'd never said as much directly, they'd been heartbroken when Sara left, and Alma knew they wouldn't last her leaving, too. The thought had been nothing but selfish impulse, the sort of thing she could see even then she would find unforgivable in herself later.

Alma found a set of clean sheets at the bottom of the trunk and stood to shake them open, billowing the fabric out over the bed. "Let me help with that," Charlie said, and he set his suitcase on the floor and crossed the room to stand opposite her, on the other side of the bed. He took the corner of the sheet and stretched it tight, tucked his side under the top, then the bottom, corners of the mattress.

"You don't have to help," Alma said. "You're a guest."

"Not true." Charlie smiled. "Family can't be guests." He tugged the edge of the sheet until it pulled neat across the mattress, then helped Alma with the blanket and quilt.

He had aged in the years since Alma had seen him. At his wedding, he wore a blue tuxedo with a white shirt that bloomed in ruffles at his chest. He was thin and wiry, and kept his hair long in those days, the length of it often pulled back into a braid that Alma believed he grew to make up for the way he otherwise faded into near invisibility, the braid his one distinguishing feature until he met Sara. She supposed this was what her sister liked about him—Sara, who felt that she shone at his side, who relished his grateful, fawning attentions. Sara, who had never blended into the crowd of other children at school or at church, who spoke too certainly and had grown up demanding her own way with a temper that other children learned to avoid. *She can't help how she is,* Alma always told herself, but within her chest she felt a white fizz of fury, a mean streak of resentment at the way Sara refused to simply fit in—resentment at the others for not simply understanding that Sara was special.

Now Charlie looked softened and eased. His hair had grayed and he'd cut it short and combed it with a part on the left side that gave his face the look of being slightly off-center, crooked but at least distinct. When he smiled, he revealed teeth yellowed by years of coffee drinking—a front tooth chipped and never repaired. And his body had slackened, his waist widened, and his shoulders stooped when he walked. As he helped make the bed, Alma saw that his movements were slow and deliberate, as if he'd perhaps developed a weak back over the years.

"This was her room," he said. "I remember it different."

"I repainted," Alma said. She turned and gathered the pillows from where she had set them on the chair in the corner, situated them on the bed against the headboard. "It was yellow before. Not yellow like a sunny kitchen, but yellow like a jaundiced baby. Yellow was Sara's color, not mine, and I didn't think I needed to look at it myself anymore if she wasn't going to, so I painted it white. Like the rest of the rooms." Alma beat the side of her hand against the pillows, fluffing them.

"She was glad you were here to take over—when they went," Charlie said. "I remember her saying she didn't like the idea of the old house gone to someone not family. It bothered her."

"Well," Alma said. "Someone needed to." She stood straight and looked at him, but he had turned to pick up the suitcase, which he set on the bed and opened, began unpacking. She might have left the room, but instead sat in the chair, watched him take the pressed squares of his shirts and slacks and shorts from the suitcase and place them in separate piles on the mattress before moving to the bureau, opening the drawers to be sure they were empty. She was surprised at his tidiness, and pleased by it. She hadn't figured him for a neat man, but maybe living with her mess of a sister had forced it.

She had not pulled the curtains on the window, had not closed the window itself, and from outside there was the sound of the tide coming in—the heavy rushing. Alma thought of the tide rolling in like blankets being pulled up for the night, one after the next after the next, until the beach was bundled, smothered. When she turned her head toward the window, she could see the lights of other houses down the beach, bright but distant across the dark spread of sand and water.

"You should fish while you're here," Alma said. "I kept the boat after Daddy died. It's in the shed behind the house. You'd have to use the truck to tug it out. It's not in prime condition by any means, but it would still float, I'm sure."

"Oh, I don't fish," Charlie said. "I never did. Maybe a little on the river at home—catfish and bluegill and whatnot to eat when I was a kid—but not for enjoyment." He picked up each pile of clothes and set them in the drawers of the bureau, smoothing his palms over the fabric before closing the drawers.

"I'll go with you," Alma said. "I haven't for years, but why not now?"

"Well," Charlie said. He seemed to hesitate, and Alma wasn't sure if it was the fishing or her he couldn't decide about.

"It was just a thought," Alma said. "I certainly have enough to get done around here if you'd rather not."

"No," Charlie said. "No, if you want to come along, in that case, I guess I could go. Sure. I could go." He smiled. "I'd be happy to go with you."

A small rush of wind gusted at the window so that the curtains lifted for a moment and then fell—so that the white scalloped edge of the quilt on the bed stirred.

"Fine," Alma said. "We'll take the boat out." She nodded her good night then and left him alone in Sara's room.

Downstairs in her own bedroom a few moments later, she could hear him still shuffling around on the floor above her, his feet in socks now, but heavy just the same, as if he were all heels. She heard him open and close the bathroom door, and then the sound of water running from the faucet in the sink.

She wondered about his life in Indiana without Sara. She wondered if he had another lady friend already, or if maybe he was the sort to go to a tavern after work, sit at the bar and drink beer pulled from the tap while he waited for the waitress to talk to him. She tried to picture Charlie Dunne flirting with an Indiana waitress, writing his phone number on the diagonal across a damp bar napkin, but the image didn't seem likely.

He no longer had the house—he had said that. He lived in an apartment in one of those complexes—a place with well-kept lawns and cheerful manufactured signs along the narrow lanes between parking lots that said things like *Welcome Home!* and *Have a Great Day!* Alma could imagine him in his apartment reading late into the night. He liked to read—Sara had mentioned it once—and Alma figured him reading the heavy novels, like *Moby-Dick* maybe, or something else long and dense and difficult, rather than the paperback detective stories she herself liked to read now and then. She could see him sitting up in the big bed he'd shared with Sara, a book in his lap and the bedside lamp on. She wondered: Had he moved all of Sara's things—her clothes and her knickknacks and the set of blue dishes Alma helped her pick out at Dietrich's department store downtown before their wedding? Or were these things gone—in boxes in a storage unit somewhere, or sold in a garage sale along with the lawn mower he would no longer need, the barbecue and the rake? All the remnants left at the end of a life. All the things made useless by loss.

There was a knock on her bedroom door, and then Lovisa appeared in the door frame. "I'm here," she said. She leaned her weight against the door and slouched. Her hair was limp, as if James's hands had been in it all night. "I just wanted to tell you," Lovisa said. "Since you seem to like to know."

"It's past midnight," Alma said, but she motioned for Lovisa to cross the room, then reached up to smooth Lovisa's hair, brushing it behind the girl's shoulders. Alma could smell the wet scent of night air on her clothes, and cigarette smoke, and the sweetly sour teenage smell of her skin. Lovisa had worn jeans and sandals with tall heels, and Alma could see that the straps of the sandals had bitten into the skin of her ankles, had rubbed what would be a blister across each of her big toes. Lovisa was pretty, though. She had Alma's blonde hair and, yes, Sara's fine coloring, Sara's taller build.

"Mom," Lovisa said, impatient. She stepped away from Alma's grasp and ruffled her hands through her hair, messing it again. "Leave me."

It was like this between them now that Lovisa was engaged, nineteen, and determined to prove her adulthood. She would let Alma hold her only a moment before she seemed to remember herself and pull away. As a girl, she'd clung to her mother, refusing to sit in her own seat at the dinner table for a time because she preferred instead to sit on Alma's lap, to eat from Alma's plate. And she was thirteen, at least, before she stopped crawling into Alma's bed after a nightmare or during a storm. *It's just you and me,* Alma had often said to her then. *Two peas in a pod we are.*

"Charlie Dunne's shown up today," Alma said. "Your aunt's husband. Her widower. You're sharing a bathroom, so keep that in mind." Alma closed the magazine she been skimming through and set it on the night table.

Lovisa stood still at her side a moment more. "What does he say about her?" she asked. "Do you think he looks ruined?"

"Good night now," Alma said. "There's no romance in a dead wife." She reached to turn off her lamp and waited for Lovisa to leave.

In a moment, she could hear her daughter climbing the stairs, crossing the floor upstairs as she prepared for sleep. Next week the house would be silent by this time each night, the only noise that of the floorboards settling, the automatic on and off of the refrigerator in the kitchen, the bundling sound of waves beyond the window. Alma moved her body beneath the blankets and pulled them up over her shoulder, up high against her neck, her face, until she felt swaddled, then she closed her eyes for sleep.

Charlie was an early riser, and in the morning Alma walked into the kitchen to find him already sitting at the table with Lovisa, the two of them eating the pancakes that Charlie had made and sharing the paper.

"So you've met," Alma said.

"You slept so late, we're old friends now," Charlie teased, and across the table Lovisa laughed and pushed a bite of pancake through the pool of syrup on her plate.

"He makes better breakfasts than you've ever made, anyway," Lovisa said, then turned to Charlie. "Seriously. My mom can't make toast. You ought to stay on and help her cook. After I leave, she might starve."

Alma flushed. "Lovisa," she said. She turned her back to them to pour her coffee, then stood at the counter, looking out the window at the beach as she drank it. Behind her, she heard Charlie fold his section of the paper once and then again, and there was the quiet clatter of Lovisa finishing her pancake, setting her fork against her plate.

"I was just joking, Mom," Lovisa said. "You know I was joking." She stood from her chair and came to the sink, bumping Alma's hip with her own by way of apology as she set her plate beneath the faucet to rinse. "You'll be fine, I know. I think you're the only person I know who's never needed anyone's help with anything."

Lovisa washed her plate and set it in the dish drainer. "I have to run," she said. She leaned and kissed Alma's cheek quickly, thanked Charlie for the food, and disappeared up the stairs.

At the counter, Alma slid two slices of bread into the toaster and waited for them to brown, then carried them on her plate to the table. Across from her, Charlie had the local news page open. "You did a good job with her," he said from behind the newsprint. "I can tell she's a good kid." He folded the paper closed and stood up, washed his plate and dried it, and left Alma to her breakfast alone.

For the next few days Charlie fit himself into their lives as if he'd always been there. Alma put him to use around the house while she worked to piece together Lovisa's wedding dress. The third porch step was loose out back, and she thought they might need to clean the gutters of the winter debris that had collected, take a trash sack out to the beach for any rubbish that had blown in. There were orders downtown for tables and chairs to be brought into the house for the reception, and the furniture needed to be relocated to make room. Charlie lugged in boxes of rented dishes and set them on the counter in the kitchen and washed them; he took his car down to the liquor store and picked up a case of champagne and a keg.

All the while, Alma sat at the kitchen table in front of the Singer, the tiny light of the machine's carriage casting a beam onto the plane of satin that she moved an inch at a time beneath the foot and needle. The dress had a fitted bodice that required several seams, a pair of lace sleeves that she fit into the holes she'd left at the shoulders, a short train onto which she would have to hand-stitch just under one hundred plastic pearls. As she worked, she let the fabric of the skirt spill over the tabletop and onto her lap, a slippery sheet of satin that was surprisingly heavy, a burden to untangle herself from each time she had to stand, rising to stretch her legs or to search out a new spool of thread.

At lunchtime she shut off the machine and got up, went to the refrigerator for bologna, mustard, and four slices of white bread that she made into sandwiches that she and Charlie ate standing at the kitchen counter.

He ate quickly and then was quiet as he waited for her to finish, too.

"It was me who always cooked," he said finally, the second day they'd eaten together. "All three meals. Sara never could get the hang of it." He ran his finger along his empty sandwich plate, collecting crumbs. "She liked spaghetti and enchiladas, and now and then a piece of steak with some asparagus on the side—fresh, not jarred. The jarred stuff is sloppy. It might as well be mush."

Beside him, Alma finished her sandwich. "She always got away with things no one else would," Alma said. Then, looking to Charlie, added, "Like the cooking. Most women cook. They have to. I always did—after Mother got too old for it, anyway, I did. Though Lovisa's right about me being no good at it really."

Through the kitchen windows, Alma could see that the tide was out, the beach extended and flat, the sky clouded over but white and bright enough to make her squint, to cause a sear of pain to flash through the nerves behind her eyes until she looked away. "Sara got away with things," she said again.

"I suppose she did," Charlie said. He reached into his back pocket where he'd tucked the baseball cap he'd been wearing all morning, and put it on. "I guess it didn't matter much, though, did it? She still wasn't happy."

"Unhappy is just another way to say spoiled."

Charlie looked at Alma for a moment. "You knew a different Sara," he said. He nodded to himself then and opened the back door. "I'll go see about those gutters," he told her over his shoulder as he walked out.

In high school, Sara had kept several boyfriends, while Alma had none. Sara was the younger sister, but more precocious, and certainly more beautiful. She wore her red hair long and went to bed each night with curlers rolled into it, so that in the mornings her hair hung in waves that bounced as she walked to school a few feet ahead of Alma, her skirt swinging an easy rhythm against the pale backs of her thighs.

The boyfriends were nameless now in Alma's mind—a Jeff, maybe, and a Ron. A boy who had a motorcycle Alma wasn't meant to know about but which she had heard rumbling beneath her window late at night when he dropped Sara off. After that, once Sara knew Alma had seen the bike, she invited Alma out with them on a Friday to eat clam strips and fries at the fish shop down the beach, and then the boyfriend built a bonfire out of driftwood, and they sat and watched it burn. He got on the bike at one point and tried to drive it along the beach, but the wheels simply spun themselves into ruts in the damp sand, and he had to tip the bike onto its side to drag it free.

He was a dark-haired boy with a thick body and a face almost too pretty to still be masculine. His eyes were damp and pale blue enough to seem nearly white at times, when he looked over at Alma there beside her sister on the sand. And after the sky went purple and ashy with dusk, he offered Alma his coat, because Sara had a sweater but Alma hadn't brought one. At the end of the night, he walked them back to the house, and Alma turned her back so he could kiss her sister at the door, heard the sound of his breath as he pulled away from Sara—a deep exhale that came out ragged.

Sara didn't see him again, though. "He was boring," she said when Alma asked about it.

They were walking home from school, and the wind that blew in off the beach gusted so that Sara had to hold her skirt in place. The wind rushed at Alma's face so that her hair snarled wildly in front of her eyes, blinding her to her next step.

He'd tried to talk her into seeing only him, Sara said. She shrugged. And he'd expected things of her—just like everyone else.

Alma had wanted to hit her sister just then, a fist across the cheek or in the gut. But it would have been impossible to actually strike Sara, and so she buried her hand in the pocket of her coat and held it there, her fingers folded into her palm like an animal into its shell.

Before the wedding dress could be completed, Alma called Lovisa downstairs for a fitting. Lovisa stood on the wooden footstool Alma usually kept in the pantry closet for reaching the high shelves, the dress's train splayed out on the floor behind her in a wide half-moon of satin. The edges were rough still, the straps of Lovisa's slip visible where the lace yoke and puffed sleeves would be attached later, and there was extra fabric at the waist and the bust. Alma knelt before her daughter, bit down on a row of pins, and began to set a hem.

"Not too short," Lovisa said. Each time she moved, Alma had to pull the pin she had just placed, readjust the fold. "I'll be wearing heels, remember. And I don't want my feet to show. I want it to look like I'm floating."

"Floating," Alma said behind her bite.

Beneath the dress now, Lovisa's feet were bare. She had painted her toenails a shade of deep red, the polish sloppy on the smaller toes and smudged where Lovisa had failed to control the little brush. She had wide feet and short toes, and when Alma looked at them she thought of Lovisa's father. She tried not to remember much about him—he was in her life for only a very short time, after all, and even then, he had seemed to her lacking, not what she had imagined for herself. When he kissed her, she shut her eyes, and her mind became a blank, white space. When she lay beside him on the narrow twin bed in his rented room downtown, she became nothing but a body.

She knew the shape of his hands, though—rough fingertips that smelled of the cedar shingles he nailed to roofs all day—his stout legs and his feet. He never dressed after he rolled away from her and got up to get a glass of water or turn on the television set against the far wall, and Alma lay still, following his feet across the room to the kitchenette, watching the way he crossed his legs at the ankle like a woman when he sat down bare to eat a sandwich at the table.

"Don't you want your pants?" she finally asked once. And he laughed, called her a prude.

When she told him later there would be a baby, he said only that he couldn't believe it—he couldn't believe she would do that to him. She got her coat then and walked out into the cool night air beyond his door, relieved to have a reason to stop seeing him, to stop feeling grateful for his small attentions, to stop wishing him better than he was.

Now, in the front room, she placed the last pin and dropped the hem of the dress over Lovisa's feet again. "Look in the mirror," she said. "Tell me if that's right by your idea of it."

Lovisa stepped down from the stool and moved to stand in front of the mirror Alma had brought down from her bedroom. She paused and smoothed the satin of the skirt, shifted slightly so that she could see the pool of the train gathered behind her.

Alma had sewn the same dress for Sara—the waistline a little tighter, the sleeves a bit more pronounced, but the cut and style the same. Sara had looked better in it than Lovisa, Alma could already see, but she guessed now that the look of things didn't matter much when it came down to it.

"Are you happy with it?" Alma asked. "If you're not, now's the time to say."

Lovisa turned and she smiled, said it was all exactly what she'd pictured it would be.

The day of Lovisa's wedding, Alma woke early and found Charlie already sitting at the kitchen table, coffee made and a mug waiting for her on the counter, a breakfast of eggs and toast and bananas cut into browning circles and wrapped beneath plastic on a plate. There was a dollop of salsa beside the eggs, and the toast had been buttered. Upstairs, Lovisa was awake and in the bathroom, the shower running so that the pipes clanked and sounded inside the walls throughout the house.

"Your eggs are probably still warm under there," he said as Alma filled her mug.

Alma peeled away the plastic, nudged the eggs with her finger, and looked at the squares of green pepper in the salsa. "Gourmet," she said, and opened the microwave, set the plate inside to reheat.

Alma had finished the wedding dress late the night before and had not yet cleared the table of the sewing machine and scissors, the remnant fabric, which lay in odd pieces about the tabletop, the edges of the satin fraying and uneven. The dress itself hung in the front room on the form, the seams already pressed flat and the buttons done up in back, ready to be undone again and fitted around Lovisa's body.

"I believe she thinks this will be the best day of her life," Alma said, and moved to the table with her mug and her plate, waited as Charlie reached forward to push aside a pile of satin scraps and make room for her.

"That would be too bad," Charlie said. "Not to be happy on your wedding day—that's not what I mean. It's just, I always thought those were the sorriest lot in high school—the ones who seemed to have their heyday before even turning twenty." He turned his mug around and around in the circle of his hands. "I'm not saying that I have a whole lot to get up to every morning now, but you hate to think you've spent it all so early." He smiled.

Alma smiled back. She sipped from her coffee and looked out through the kitchen window to where the sky was just paling, fading to a gray the color of soot. It had rained in the night, and she knew if she stood and opened the back door and stepped out onto the wet planks of the porch, the air would smell of rain—of damp driftwood and sand. Of things softening—the wood siding of the house and the roof, the fibers of the clusters of sea grass beyond the porch steps. Whenever it rained, several of the fronds broke or bent, and the beach was littered with the flotsam of the storm—the red noodles and bulbs of kelp that washed to shore; bits of driftwood and branches blown down from further up the beach; paper plates and plastic sacks, dented soda and beer cans. All these things wasted by the rain and the wind, half buried in the sand and made part of the beach.

"She'll be up there in Alaska on her own," Alma said. She moved the eggs across her plate. "I don't know, though. Maybe she'll be okay. Some people know how to be alone without getting worn out with loneliness."

Across the table, Charlie shook his head. "I don't know who."

He looked as if he expected Alma to reach for his hand, to sympathize. She had seen her father look the same way, after her mother's death—had seen him wait for women at the church or the coffee shop downtown to offer him their pity, to cluck over him, the widower, as if he were a child abandoned. There were those who believed that such a loss was unendurable for a man—the same women who liked to stop by unannounced on a Saturday afternoon to drop off a casserole dish and a strawberry pie "for Mr. Lindquist's supper," to sit and have a cup of coffee with him while Alma went ahead with the laundry and the bill paying and the rest of the Saturday tasks that needed to be done whether or not one felt grieved or lonely or cheated.

"You know, I almost left before our wedding," Charlie said. "Mine and Sara's. The night before, I almost got on the bus then and left. Your folks had a dinner—you remember it? You sat by her. You touched her hair at one point. Like a mother touches a baby, and that's how you looked at her, too. You seemed protective." Charlie placed his hands flat on the table again, as he had the other day. "I wasn't sure I could say she meant as much to me then—not as much as she meant to you."

They sat without speaking, the light outside the window brighter now and hard white with morning.

"You weren't good enough for her," Alma said. "That's what I thought then. I was surprised she chose you."

Alma drank the last of the coffee in her cup. "There will be guests soon," she said, and she pushed back in her chair, stood and left him.

It was early afternoon when Charlie asked her to clip his hair. The ends were beginning to get a little long, to curl at his neck in a way he thought looked raggedy for a wedding, and so he came downstairs just after lunch carrying a shaving kit, and from it pulled a tiny pair of scissors meant for trimming a mustache.

"These will never work," Alma said. Her face had flushed when he'd asked for her help, and she turned away to find a pair of old sewing shears in the drawer in the kitchen. She rummaged through the mess of envelopes and paper clips and cap-less pens until she felt sure her color had faded, then held up the shears and faced him.

Charlie carried a towel over his shoulder, and when he sat in one of the kitchen chairs, his back to Alma, he flapped the towel out around his back like a cape, grasping its ends at his neck.

His neck was pale, the skin creased deeply, and Alma fumbled to fold down his shirt collar, to tuck it into itself. She held the blades of the shears flat against his head then, at the soft slope where his neck began, and cut away the curls in short, mindful clips.

"I might have gone to a barber," Charlie said. "I didn't think of it until now."

"No matter," Alma said. "I can do it."

"Do you have any hair-cutting experience to make me feel a little better about this?"

"I used to trim Lovisa's bangs, when she was small. She hated it. She wriggled and the cut always came out crooked."

"I guess I'll sit still, then," Charlie said. He laughed, and Alma finished the cut in careful order, set the shears on the tabletop and pulled away the towel, brushed her fingers against the back of his neck to sweep away any trimmings. She felt awkward touching his skin, as if it were a trespass, and so she made her movements brusque, terse.

"I've got the floor," Charlie said when he stood. He gathered the towel in his arms, held his shaving kit beneath his elbow.

"It's fine," Alma said, though, and when he left she went to the closet for the broom and swept the floor beneath the chair, then carried the clippings in the dustpan to the porch, where she shook them out onto the sand. She thought of the birds that would search out and collect these bits of Charlie's hair—not beach birds, but sparrows and robins and the gray-bellied birds she couldn't name. She imagined his hair woven into nests beneath the bramble of blackberry across the road and tucked under the branches of the box hedges that lined the front yards of houses in town. Hair knitted into the nests of this place along with strings of fishing line and feathers, strands of sea grass and the fibers of her own drier lint, picked from the vent outside the house and carried away in small beaks like treasure.

By three o'clock the rented chairs had been arranged on the beach and the guests had been seated. Alma stood in the kitchen waiting for Lovisa to appear at the staircase in her dress, her girlfriends in tow, all alike in their yellow dresses, all giggling as they had been throughout the day behind Lovisa's bedroom door. Alma would be seated last, Lovisa had told her; James would be her escort. Once she was seated, the bridesmaids would descend the wooden steps of the porch and make their way to the minister and James, and then Lovisa would walk alone toward her groom. Alma and Lovisa had been disagreeing about this for weeks—Alma arguing that someone should be found to walk with Lovisa, even though that someone couldn't be her father. But Lovisa was stubborn, and Alma gave in, finally, only just before the service.

"I'd be happy to do the honors," Charlie had offered. "I know I'm not a father or a grandfather or anything, but maybe I'll do." He had brought a jacket he could run upstairs and put on, he said. He'd be presentable.

Lovisa thanked him but insisted: She would walk alone.

The absence of any father to escort Lovisa seemed an impropriety to Alma—an embarrassment. Just another reminder that her life had not quite gone as she might have hoped.

Looking out at the rows of seated guests—cousins and acquaintances from the church, people Alma had known since she was a child—she searched out Charlie and spotted him in the second row of seats. He wore his suit and held himself stiffly in it, upright and maybe proud. Alma could imagine him as someone's father. She wouldn't have said that when he first married Sara—Charlie with the long hair and the jeans. But she felt now that he might have been cheated out of fatherhood, choosing her sister as his wife.

After Lovisa was born, the day that Alma packed her suitcase with the intention of leaving—leaving the baby to her parents, getting on a bus and going east—she called Sara.

"How is the baby?" Sara said into the phone before Alma could begin, could say that she was coming out, that she'd made up her mind.

There was the sound of distance on the phone line between them—a thinning of Sara's voice and a lag of a second or two between her sentences. Time enough for Alma to imagine Sara's words moving across the span of the whole country, bits of words like a dry, shifting snow passing through the white atmosphere above the clouds.

But before Alma could answer, Sara went on. "I can't believe you have a baby," she said. "There goes the rest of your life." She snuffed slightly on the other end of the line, and then there was the dry crackle of a pause. "I shouldn't have said that. I'm sure she's a beautiful baby. Still, I just can't believe you let it happen."

Later, in another month or two, when Lovisa was baptized, there was a card in the mail from Indiana. Sara had signed only her name, but beneath her signature, Charlie had printed his name as well, and in his hand the words *Joy! Joy!*

Alma thought it a strange thing to write—too Christmassy. Those two exclamation points overly exuberant and the sentiment likely false, the sort of thing one writes because something happy must be written.

She was warmed a little, though, and slid the card back into its envelope, placed it behind a plastic sheet on one of the pages of the baby book she'd begun for Lovisa.

In the kitchen now, James arrived at the doorway and offered Alma his arm. He smelled boyish still—his aftershave too strong—and he was sweating, a line of perspiration beaded along his hairline. Alma could hear his breath coming quickly as she took his arm and let him lead her past the guests to her seat in the first row, there in front of Charlie, who reached forward and layed his hand on her shoulder, gave a squeeze just as James left her, and the whole congregation on the beach rose, turned their faces toward the house where Lovisa appeared in her white dress, the bride now, ready to be married.

* * *

James and Lovisa left just after the cake was served, James hoisting Lovisa over his shoulder—the way he might lift a net of stinky fish on his boat, Alma thought—and carrying her out to the car. Lovisa waved at the crowd of guests and at her mother, her face bright with the heat of her own excitement, the flush of her own possibility, as if Alaska were a wonderland instead of just another state, farther north. Alma turned away then and did not move with the rest of the party out to the front to watch them drive off.

Soon enough, everyone else had gone as well, and the house was empty and quiet by early evening. Alma moved through the front room collecting discarded paper plates and the plastic champagne flutes the guests had used to toast the newlyweds. On one of the tables, someone had left her purse, a pair of glasses on another table, a silk scarf that lay in a heap on the floor, wrinkling. And there were wadded napkins to be tossed out, uneaten wedding cake, plastic cups of beer that had sat warming, brewing a pale, yeasty scent that made the room stuffy and stale and suddenly dizzying. Alma set down the plates she had in her hands and walked out through the kitchen to stand on the porch for just a moment, to catch her breath, and was there when Charlie opened the door. Above his head, the porch light was on, and the blued and dusty bodies of moths bumped against its bulb, batting clumsy arcs away from and back to its heat.

"I was thinking of your offer," Charlie said. "To take the boat out. We should do that now." He stood straight. He had taken off his jacket and unbuttoned the top buttons of his shirt so that the neck of his undershirt was visible. He had rolled up his sleeves to his elbows. "Let's just leave this mess for later," he said.

He waited for Alma to change out of her dress and into a pair of jeans, and then they crossed the yard to the shed. The boat was nothing but a wooden skiff, wide bodied but not big, the blue paint peeling in curls from its sides. It did not take Charlie long to start up the old truck and fix the boat trailer to the bumper, tug the boat the short distance to the shoreline. Alma found the oars behind the shed door and brought them down, and then they left the truck, the trailer's back wheels not quite submerged in the tide, and climbed into the boat and pushed off.

The water was easy, the waves manageable with just the two oars. They sat together at the boat's center, and at first they tried to coordinate their strokes, but finally fell into a lopsided rhythm that carried them slowly out away from the beach. Alma appreciated the work of the rowing after the long day, the strained pull in her arms when she reached against the waves. Her long sleeves tugged at the shoulders, and Sara's ring on its chain bumped against her chest beneath her shirt as she moved.

Above the boat, the sky was shadowing with night but was not yet dark, and the clouds stretched thin and gauzy. The water was the color of charcoal—black enough to swallow the blade of Alma's oar completely each time it dipped beneath the surface.

They stopped rowing when it became work and just sat, Alma's underarms damp with perspiration and Charlie out of breath, the cuffs of his pants and his shoes wet from unloading the boat from the trailer. More water now sloshed gently at their feet.

"The boat leaks," Charlie said. "You didn't tell me you planned to drown me out here."

Alma laughed. "The leaking will stop when the wood swells. I promise we won't sink. But you've ruined those." She nodded to his shoes. "They'll smell like the sea."

"I bought them for her funeral," he said. "But then decided not to hold one. I'll probably never wear them again, anyway."

Alma held her oar, watching the rings it sent raying out across the dark water slide one into the next into the next, slipping shape. "I want to know about that," she said. "I thought I'd be polite and not ask, but there it is."

Charlie shrugged. "You were there for your mother," he said. "I'm sure you remember well enough."

"Yes. I suppose I can imagine."

"Sara wasn't good at dying," he said. "Some people find a way to go gracefully—or so I hear—but your sister couldn't. She wasn't so much in discomfort at the end as she was sorry for herself." He paused. "She said one night that she was disappointed about her life being what it was, and no chance to change it now. I don't know what that meant. That she'd expected more, I guess. Sometimes I think about it, and it bothers me."

The tide was carrying them in again, and so they lifted their oars and rowed out a few feet farther.

Alma imagined her sister's body on the metal table of a mortuary. Sara like a mannequin. She wasn't certain—did they fix the body before cremation? Did they comb her hair and brush her teeth? Fit clothes around her frame and put shoes on her feet? Did someone see to it that she did not slide into the afterlife—whatever it might be—without attention to these things? That she was not permitted to leave this world entirely untended?

Beneath her, Alma felt the unbalancing motion of the waves, the slapping of water to wood, and she leaned into Charlie, put her arms around him in an awkward sort of hug. He tucked his forehead into the bend of her neck, so that she could feel the warmth of him, could smell the sweet brown scent of beer still on his breath when he exhaled.

Across the black, shifting body of the water, the house sat removed, a place foreign to her but familiar, the lamps still lit and the door still open on the back porch. The curtains were drawn at the windows, and Alma could see inside to the tables and the chairs, the white bunches of peonies the bridesmaids had carried sitting in vases now along the windowsill. The flowers had looked like handfuls of snow in the girls' bouquets that afternoon—smaller versions of the bouquet Lovisa had thrown over her head just before leaving the reception. It had lost petals when she tossed it—a pretty snow of white—and Alma had thought of the day she'd packed to leave the baby Lovisa so many years before, thought of the thick tights and winter coat she had rolled into the suitcase's satin pocket in anticipation of traveling to someplace colder, someplace that would release her from here. She had thought then that she could board a bus and get away with simply leaving. What had turned her around? She couldn't remember now. The sense of obligation she couldn't deny. The maternal responsibility. Yes, she had felt those things, but also fear. Alma could imagine her life in Indiana with Sara, but she had no idea what lay ahead for her here, with Lovisa. She had no idea how life would turn out if she stayed, and she was afraid to miss the things she couldn't yet see.

In the boat Alma sat up but slipped her hand beneath Charlie's, felt the cool of his grasp and the knit of his fingers between hers as he held to her.

"I wasn't sure I should come out for this visit," Charlie said.

"No." Alma shook her head. "It was her wedding, and you're family. It was good of you to come."

"You ought to come my way next time," Charlie said. "I mean it. I'd be glad to see you again."

"I will," Alma told him. "I always meant to."

They sat still for another moment, until the last of the light drained over the bowed line of the horizon and the sky and the water were one continuous swath. Then, beginning to chill, they picked up the oars and rowed back toward the shore, toward the house and its warmth.

CARMEL

HE DOES NOT WANT TO LEAVE HIS WIFE. This much seems clear as Graham navigates the rental car around the soft bends of Highway 1, Sophie in the passenger seat at his side, her head against the window and her eyes shut as if she is asleep. The sun is full in her window, and the bangles on her wrist catch the light, webbing a pattern on the car's windshield, the roof, the dash. Beyond her window, the road drops off in a sharp series of brown bluffs that end several hundred feet below in the Pacific Ocean. When Graham looks at her, all he can see is the spread of that water, an impossible shade of blue today that strikes him as beautifully unreal—like the color of gaudy turquoise stones, or of Hollywood movie oceans, or of their hotel's swimming pool.

It was Graham who convinced Sophie to join him on this trip—a conference in Carmel titled "The Aesthetics of Landscape Photography in the Age of Technology." He teaches the classic stuff—the history of photography, the early masters—and knew from the start that the conference would likely leave him feeling old and outmoded. But a week away from the Chicago cold on the department's budget sounded good. They could consider it a vacation. How long had it been since their last vacation? Maybe that was all she needed—rest. She could lie out by the pool and sun herself while he attended the morning seminars. She could come to the evening cocktail parties with him if she liked, and in between lectures and panels, they could sightsee, rent a car and drive up the coast to Monterey, or south to San Simeon if she wanted, to that castle. He had heard zoo animals still roamed the property there, just off the highway—zebras standing in the shade of planned oak groves and eucalyptus trees as if they were natives, tamed lions stalking through the blond grass of the hillsides. It would be something to see.

He bought her plane ticket before she could say no, and now here she is beside him.

When he woke up this morning, the day had seemed to hold so much promise. He had slept the kind of deep sleep he rarely slept anymore—sleep without dreams or interruptions—so that when he opened his eyes he was pleasantly disoriented for a moment, unable to quite remember the circumstances of his life beyond this room. Only early March, yet there was the white eight o'clock light coming through the sheer curtains at the open window as if it were summer already, and the California scent of orange blossoms on the breeze; the happy, shallow sound of a swimmer in the pool below—arms and legs and face dipping beneath the water and then coming up again with small splashes. Graham pushed himself to sitting against the headboard. He felt cheerful for the first time in a long time.

At home, Sophie kept heavy drapes on the bedroom window, convinced the neighbors might otherwise be tempted to peep. She liked the room dark and quiet and cool, and when Graham woke in the morning, it was often to the harsh sound of her filling the tub in the adjoining bathroom, the water raging against the enamel tub basin, and a thin line of light and steam creeping out from around the shut door.

This morning, though, he woke to her lying beside him, still and sleeping. He leaned over her and kissed her cheek so that she stirred, yawned, opened her eyes. "It's morning," he said. He wanted to touch her shoulder, the pale rim of her collarbone, but he knew he should wait until she gave him some sign or she would be irritated, thinking he was pushing himself on her.

"I was sleeping." She rolled away from him, pulling the sheet to her chin. "You said this would be a vacation."

Graham got up and went into the bathroom, showered and shaved and brushed his teeth, pulled a linen shirt and a pair of shorts from his suitcase and dressed, then slid his room card into his pocket. At the door, he stopped and turned to look at her. She had her eyes closed again but wasn't sleeping. "I'm going to breakfast now, Sophie," he said. He stood looking at her. "I wish you would dress yourself before I come back." He waited, and when she didn't blink or move, Graham went out into the hallway and took the elevator to the lobby, where a continental breakfast of biscuits and spotty bananas and a basket of jams was set out on a folding table near the silver coffee carafes and the bowl of single-serving creamers.

He began to wish he had not brought her. He had been to plenty of these conferences alone, and though the speakers were unfailingly dull and the panels generally useless, there would have been relief in being apart from her. He could have got up in that pale light of morning and held on to the sense of the day as open to him. He could have enjoyed the breakfast he was about to have; could have spent the afternoon swimming tidy laps back and forth along the length of the pool and come inside in the evening, contented by the exertion of his swimming and ready to sit down to dinner, to stay up late drinking at the bar with the other professors, having the sort of conversation about his work and his interests that she never tolerated.

"Your friends are stuffy," she'd said last night when he'd persuaded her to have just one drink before bed.

"They're colleagues, not friends," he defended himself, but she went on.

"I don't know how you can stand one another. Honestly. I don't know how you convince yourselves that all that talk amounts to a heap of anything." She stood before the mirror in the bathroom, pulling the pins from her hair so that it fell down her back. She'd taken off her dress when they walked into the room, and it lay wrinkling on the floor at the foot of the bed, her heels by the door where she had stepped out of them. At the mirror, she was in just her slip, the backs of her thighs exposed, and her skin there marbled by purple veins and slightly dimpled just below her backside. It had been some time since Graham had seen her legs bare, and he preferred to think of them as they had been when he'd met her—smooth and firm and unblemished, like the legs of Weston's nudes, like Adams's slim white aspens.

Now, in the car beside him, Sophie raises her head. "Where are we going? Did you have a destination in mind, or are we just going to spend the day driving?"

The ocean is a blue deepening of the sky on the other side of her window, like a trompe l'oeil. Like one of those pen and ink drawings Graham finds difficult to look at—a floor merging with a ceiling, a window that should look out instead looking in.

"We'll get there," he says.

Beyond his window, the elongated shadows of the sycamores and sequoias stretch across the roadway and shade the pavement, dappling the light coming in through the windshield so that it flickers and jumps, and Graham has to squint to see. He takes his hands off the wheel for a moment, steadily steering with his knee, then removes his sunglasses and wipes the lenses with the hem of his shirt.

"Imagine living here," Sophie says. "Imagine living where it's sunny every day—even Christmas. Sun on Christmas." She shifts, leans her head back against the seat and closes her eyes again. She always looks exhausted lately. Not sleep deprived, but tired. She has not put on makeup today, and her face is pale and drawn—still pretty, but too old for her age.

"Yes," Graham says. "I suppose it would seem unnatural." He replaces his glasses on his face and makes another turn with the road.

Sophie opens her eyes now and then as they drive and glances at the strip of blue Pacific, the deep shade that falls beneath the trees along the road when the sun is as direct as it is here. It is all too much a postcard for her liking, but the truth is she isn't minding the time away from home, the change of scenery.

She's spent most of the week lying on a chaise lounge by the pool outside the hotel, the sun on her legs and her stomach, the scent of chlorine skiffing off the pool's surface and reminding her of childhood, of the summers she spent at the public pool during high school. She even thought to buy some of that lotion she used to use—greasy and smelling of coconuts—and just the smell of it made her want a raggy magazine and a cherry snow cone.

As a teenager, she'd spent nearly every day of her summer vacations at the pool. She could bike there from her parents' house, her towel rolled under one arm and her bikini already on, her long legs bare and working in quick circles as she pedaled down the residential streets toward the pool. Her awareness of her body was innocent then—her browned shoulders and slim waist, her breasts and hips and flat stomach a given. When Bradley Jones kissed her standing in line for the diving board the summer she was fifteen, she just leaned into the kiss. And when those five days came each month—predictable as school beginning again in September—she cursed herself quietly for being born female and put on a pair of cutoffs, lay around beneath the lifeguard chairs, and told her friends she was taking a break from swimming to work on her tan. She thought of her own body no differently then than she might have thought about a car or a toaster oven or a washing machine—something standard. A thing useful and necessary and easily taken for granted.

She knows better now. In the last few years, she has come to think of herself as someone living in foreign skin. She wonders if all women learn to feel this way—her aunts, and her mother, and the woman she noticed across the pool yesterday, with the baggy white T-shirt on over her suit. It is how she figures all of the unwell must feel—betrayed by their own bones.

Graham does not see it this way. After the first miscarriage, when she called his office from the bathroom, her skirt around her ankles and the pain in her middle just beginning and still mild, he said only, "Oh. Oh, I see." And then, "Well, we knew this was a risk." After the fourth, he said it was just a matter of odds—that if they kept at it, eventually percentages would be in their favor. He sees the fertility tests they've done, the laparoscopic surgery Sophie had five years ago and then again last year, as one might see dental appointments or visits to the barber: routine if unpleasant maintenance.

When he lies down beside her these days, touches her, she cannot help but wonder if he comes to bed with this same economy of emotion; if he thinks of her as that car or toaster oven—of conception as engineering, their bodies as reliable managers of the biological. It makes him culpable, a coconspirator with her body—he who can still find it desirable and trustworthy. As soon as he finishes, she rolls away, lies with her back turned to him and her eyes on the wall.

"Did you bring your suit today?" Graham asks as they drive. "I don't know if you'd want to swim in the Pacific here—it's probably so cold—but it seems you've been enjoying your swimming this week." He takes his eyes from the road quickly to look at her, smiles. "Maybe tonight, when we get back, we can do a few laps together."

He's been all false pleasantries lately. When he speaks to her this way, her patience with him thins, and she feels like an egg about to crack.

"I haven't touched the water all week," Sophie says. "I haven't done anything."

"All right, then," Graham says. He looks at her again, his expression harder, irritated—or maybe sad. She isn't sure. "We'll just find a place to pull over and eat," he says. "I'm hungry. I'm sure you must be hungry."

Sophie nods. There are moments like this between them now and then, when he seems familiar again. Moments when she recognizes his effort, and his confusion. How can he bring her back? What can he do? She knows he'd ask if he knew how.

She shuts her eyes and turns her head toward the window, but she can tell even without looking at him that Graham is still watching her as he drives, shifting his eyes her way every few moments to see if she is—what? Still conscious? Still breathing? Still the woman he married?

An honest wife would tell him, no, that girl is long gone.

In the department, people have stopped asking about Sophie's health. Graham supposes they talk about him—about his marriage—when his back is turned, and though this is embarrassing, he would rather people gossip than ask him directly how she is, force him to find an appropriate answer. In the beginning—after the first loss and then the second—he had to accept their concern. He gave Professor Gunsul his hand and let her squeeze it when she stopped him in the hallway to express her condolences. He smiled kindly when he caught Professor Thomas watching him across the seminar table at a department meeting, and nodded, gracious, to acknowledge the other man's look of pity. They were all sorry for him, sorry for their curiosity, and he understood their kindnesses to be in part their own guilt. People wanted tears, he decided. They wanted him to fall behind in his grading, to begin missing classes. They wanted him to tell them that his wife had gone to pieces, that she couldn't stop weeping, that she was inconsolable.

Someone had sent a curry casserole to the house this November, after Sophie's last stay in the hospital. Graham found the glass dish on the kitchen counter when he returned home in the evening, a note taped to the lid that read: *One gray day / Will rot even the best house a man can build . . . With deepest sympathies.* Graham turned the paper over in his hand, looking for a name on the back, but there was none.

"What is this?" he asked, carrying the note from the kitchen to the front room, where Sophie sat in the chair near the window, a blanket spread over her legs. It was almost winter—not fully cold out yet, but chilly. The leaves on the oak in the yard had already yellowed and fallen, but the shrubbery along the window was still green, the burning bush Sophie's mother had bought and planted when she'd come to stay a year ago a flaming and florescent red at the curb. "What is this?" he asked again, and he handed her the card.

"Tell your friend your wife hates sloppy poetry," Sophie said.

On the following Monday, when Professor Gunsul knocked and then poked her head around his office door to ask if the casserole had come out well when reheated, Graham simply nodded. "Thank you," he said. "It was just what we needed."

* * *

Along the highway, Graham finds a turnout and pulls onto the gravel, stops the engine. He opens his door and walks around to the trunk, fumbles to put on his jacket in the wind that blows in gusts off of the ocean, then finds the brown bags he asked the hotel kitchen to pack for him, the bottle of apple juice he paid double-price for at the desk in the lobby. He's brought one of the extra blankets from the closet in the hotel room, a yellow matted thing with a yellow satin binding, and he rolls it now and stuffs it under his arm, shuts the trunk, and walks to Sophie's door to open it for her. She has not unfastened her seat belt, and sits looking through the windshield. "Come on," he says. "I'm not leaving you on the side of the highway."

They step over the guardrail and make their way along a trail other tourists have used, the brush and the ice plant beaten back by feet, so that a sandy path weaves across a plane of rock out to a point. There are no trees growing on this side of the highway, the soil too rocky, Graham assumes. Nothing could root here. The first good storm would break any grip a tan oak or a flimsy alder had and would send it over the slope of the hillside to the tide pools below.

He stops to wait for Sophie, who is looking at the pink ice plant blooms.

"It's an invasive species," he says. "I read it in the morning paper. They want to get rid of it along the beaches because it's choking out the grasses." The plant looks to Graham like fingers—fat, ugly little spears that pink toward their ends and here and there have sent up a flower. "It's non-native," he says. "It'll kill everything else."

Sophie straightens and puts her hand to her face, shades her eyes so that she can see him. "That's ridiculous," she says, then steps ahead of him on the path, moves on her own toward the point.

It's high and breezy here, and the sea is too distant. If Graham were alone, he'd have driven farther south instead, to one of the beaches, where he could spread a towel on the sand and lie back. Or north maybe, and inland, to stop at one of the wineries for a tasting. There was a group going to do that today, and he could have tagged along. They'd invited him last night, but Sophie had turned her face to him, wrinkled her nose so only he could see. The others envied Graham because of Sophie. They smiled when she spoke and offered to buy her a drink. When she leaned forward to hear Professor Andersen over the bar's music, Graham had seen the professor's eyes flick quickly down at the V of her dress's neckline. The other wives were all older, dowdier. They had stayed home to tend to children and daily life. The professor from New Mexico—was his name Tom? Timothy?—said his wife had called; both of their boys had the stomach flu, and she'd been up all night cleaning bedsheets and getting the boys to the toilet. *I swear to you,* he'd said, *I'm so glad not to be home right now. Those boys are exhausting. I haven't slept through the night in ten years.* He laughed, and the others joined him.

Graham had reached for Sophie beneath the table then, laid his hand on her thigh, just beneath the fabric of her skirt. She was warm, and she hadn't worn stockings. He could feel the fine hairs she never shaved there, above her knee, and in the midst of the conversation he imagined her as she looked bare in the bed beside him, the long stretch of her rib cage and the sink of her stomach between the two rises of her hipbones, the length of her legs next to his own. This was a memory, though, he reminded himself—this body. When he met her, he thought of her like the art he admired, her lines and her loveliness and her limitation evident and simple, like a Modotti print, or a Cunningham nude. But she rarely let him see her unclothed now. The last time he'd seen her fully naked, in fact, was over two years ago, just before the third miscarriage. She lost that pregnancy later than the others, and so was showing already. He remembers how pleased she was with her new shape, the slight round just below her navel, and how she had stepped out of the shower one morning and stood in front of the mirror in their bedroom admiring herself. Her breasts were heavier, the nipples dark, and when he moved up behind her and put his hands to her chest—he remembers—she didn't pull away.

Graham finds a clear, flat spot on the bluff and sets down the lunch bags, shakes the blanket so that it billows and spreads out in a square on the ground. He finds four rocks and anchors the blanket's corners, sits, and opens the lunch bags, and lays out their lunch: sandwiches on thin bread, wrapped in yellow cellophane; two of the bananas he'd seen at breakfast; and a cookie each. He hasn't remembered cups, so they'll have to drink the apple juice from the bottle.

Sophie doesn't sit. She walks along the ledge of rock, leans to look out, and bends far enough that Graham gets to his knees, nearly reaches for her, then feels foolish when she turns around again. "There are tide pools," she says.

"We can drive down to them later," he tells her. "We should eat now." He unwraps his sandwich, doesn't wait any longer for her to sit. His stomach feels suddenly hollowed and hard and shrunken with hunger. He is never hungry like this at home, and he takes his appetite as a sign of the better climate here, the better air—strained by salt and scented by the eucalyptus groves and the redwoods. There is a vigor to this place that puts Graham in mind of nineteenth-century curative baths—ladies retreating to the seaside or to the soapy shores of mineral lakes to ease sciatica or hysteria or a dyspeptic stomach. He's never put any stock in those treatments, but perhaps there is something to the idea of warmer temperature and balmy sea air because he feels like a new man here, finally released from the winter and from everything. His other life at home seems pale and easily erased.

Graham finishes his sandwich, begins on his cookie, and looks to Sophie, who has crouched now and seems to be studying the tide pools below. "We should move to California," Graham says. The idea has just struck him, and he smiles. His mouth is full, and she turns to him as if she hasn't heard. "We should move here," he says again. "I'll quit at the college. It doesn't matter. We could sell the house." He can imagine himself in a bungalow near the beach, his skin browned and polished—he could do with the sun. He can picture himself happy here, a healthier, younger version of himself, and Sophie beside him, restored as well. "We could become beachcombers," he says. "You could learn to surf."

"I don't understand the point of surfing," she says. "You go out just to come back in. It's useless energy."

"No different than basketball or bicycling," Graham says. "They do it just for the sport, I think. Wouldn't you like to be out in those waves?"

"You don't play basketball, and I've never seen you ride a bike," Sophie says. She sits and eases herself over the edge of the rock until she is standing on the slope of land below. "I don't want lunch," she says. "You can eat mine, or just throw it to the gulls." For a moment, just the top of her head is visible, and then there is the sound of her feet on the gravel and the dirt as she picks her way down the hillside.

Graham knows he should stand and call her back, but he is tired. He unwraps her sandwich and eats it, finishes her cookie and both bananas. He leaves half of the juice in the bottle for her and then lies back on the blanket, toes off his shoes, and closes his eyes. The sun warms him only gradually, the light white and then silvered behind his eyelids, the sound of the water below and the wind in the trees across the road one sound—a quiet rushing, like the sound of blood moving through veins.

When he and Sophie married, Graham would never have imagined it possible for things between them to turn as they have. He met Sophie during his first term on campus; she was a graduate student, twelve years his junior. She was studying literature but had taken one of his classes on a whim, she told him the first week of the term, because the course catalog had said there would be no final. It was an undergraduate course, and she just needed to fill credits while she worked on her thesis.

Had Sophie been any one of his other students, he might have told her to drop the class while she still could, advising her to get her credits elsewhere—across campus in the theater department, maybe, or in one of those wine-tasting classes he'd heard always had a full wait list. Sophie was lovely, though—his office smelled of lavender when she left, and he found himself wondering if it was her perfume or some sort of soap. He imagined her nude in a bathtub anytime he saw her, and because of this, he blushed whenever she spoke up in class. When she appeared at his door during office hours the first time, ready to argue something he'd said during lecture, he found himself warm, nervous, the armpits of his shirt damp with perspiration. Her willingness to contest him caught Graham off guard, and pleased him. She was bright and surprising, the kind of girl he never thought would pay him any attention.

When she eventually agreed to go out with him, Graham had the same sense of giddy pleasure about finding her as he'd had finding a penny on the sidewalk as a child, as if someone—God maybe—had noticed his good behavior and had gifted him with a little token of thanks, something unexpected and probably undeserved.

They'd gone to Hawaii for their honeymoon—eight years ago already. He'd worked hard to finish the semester's classes and the grading before the wedding so he could be completely free for it, and he'd planned to just sit on the beach, to sip one of those drinks you could buy at the hotel bar and take outside—a mai tai or a daiquiri with a bamboo stake of pineapple suspended across the rim of the glass. He'd brought a novel to read.

But Sophie talked him into paying for snorkeling lessons, and so they put on suits and the ridiculous rented fins, the masks and the snorkels, and they went out with their guide to a bit of shallow water fenced off by ropes and buoys. There were starfish in purple and orange below the water—their five legs harder than he'd expected, a rigid lace raised on their skin—and bright fish and anemones opened like yellow and white thistle blossoms. Graham had to struggle to keep his body stiff and floating, the horn of his snorkel above the waterline so that he didn't draw in any of the sea. His mask fogged, and then he bumped it with an elbow trying to swim, so that water poured in and clouded his eyes until he lifted his head again, took the thing off, and swam for shore. He spent the rest of their hour standing just outside the fenced area, in the shallow, warmer water where there were little children splashing one another and squealing. When Sophie finally joined him, she snapped the waist of his swim trunks. "You're a curmudgeon," she said. "It was beautiful down there—all that going on so bright under the water where you wouldn't even notice it." She'd kissed the back of his neck, and the salt water still on her lips stung his sunburn.

He was promoted at the college and then tenured, and so they bought a house and began to settle. Sophie taught literature courses now and then, as an adjunct, and spent the rest of her time at the library. When he came home in the afternoons, he often found her bent over a stack of books at the dining table, a pencil out. She underlined what she appreciated in the text, what she wanted to read again, and then thumbed back through the pages later, erasing before returning the borrowed books. She kept a list for herself of all the books she thought she should read but never had, and as she checked them out and read them, she drew lines through their titles on her list. She'd crossed off *Anna Karenina* and *The Lover* the first year they were married, *The Diary of Anaïs Nin* the following year. She liked to read aloud to him after supper in the evenings, and Graham liked listening.

Sophie took up gardening once they bought the house as well, planting flower beds in the front yard and an herb garden near the back door. The herbs sent up a bitter smell—the odors of lemon grass and basil and thyme commingling with the dark, bodily stink of the compost in which she'd rooted the plants.

"You should cut them back," Graham said once. "The herbs. They're for cooking."

"I like my herbs leggy and awkward," she said. "Like my men." She nudged him with her elbow as she passed, gave him a look.

It seems to Graham, looking back now, that she was happy then, and he had envisioned their lives going on as they were indefinitely. Perhaps they would take a long trip during his sabbatical. They might buy each other skis one Christmas and start making a yearly vacation to the Rockies. But by their second anniversary, she was different. "There are holes in our marriage," she said one night. "It all seems like a lot of nothing." They'd been out to dinner, as had become their Friday habit, and then had come straight home, not knowing what else to do with the evening. They'd put on their pajamas, and Graham planned to read for a while before going to sleep, while Sophie sat on the edge of the bed, lotioning her legs. She pumped a great gob of lotion into her palm as she spoke, and bent now and then to slather her calves instead of looking at him. "I can't stand us," she said. "I couldn't stand us if we invited ourselves to dinner."

"That doesn't make any sense," Graham said. He stood near the bed, his robe still on over his shorts. He was tired and wanted to climb beneath the blankets, spend a few minutes with his *Newsweek* before shutting out the light and falling asleep. "We could go away for the weekend," he said. "If you want a change. I could book a hotel in the city. There's a new exhibit at the Art Institute I wanted to see. And you always like that collection of miniatures they have there."

Sophie said nothing for a moment, and then she got up and went into the bathroom, where he heard her rifling through the medicine cabinet, the squeak of the mirror closing shut and then a rattling, the tap water running in the sink. When she came back to bed, she shut off her lamp and turned away from him. "I've dumped my birth-control pills," she said. "We'll see what happens."

In the dark, Graham lay on his back with his eyes open. He heard her pass into sleep, her breathing deeper, and the breaths drawn in jagged through quiet snores. It seemed the room was impossibly dark—the darkness thick enough that when he stretched out his hand and waved it in front of his face, he couldn't see a thing.

Sophie finds her way down to the tide pools easily and then crouches beside one, slides her hand into the tepid water. Purple anemones cluster in florets along the basin, and there are limpets and mussels and barnacles as well, their shells like coins tossed into a public fountain, brown and silvered and greening there beneath the water. She stirs the pool and imagines fleshy feet grasping the rock like tiny, sucking mouths.

She expected Graham to follow her and looks up again to see if he has. She has irritated him. She has disappointed his expectations for the day. This is one of his most trying traits—this need to set a vision and adhere to it. When she met him, she found it funny, an idiosyncrasy that she thought entirely sweet. The first night she stayed at his apartment, he'd stopped their kissing on the couch and asked her to move into the bedroom, to leave her blouse on so that he could unbutton it, and she knew that he'd been planning the moment for some time, that she was part of his fantasy life. The thought charmed her, and she was suddenly calm and assured, his desire encouraging her own.

In the morning, she lay awake beside him a long time before waking him as well. His apartment was a basement unit, the bedroom window level with the sidewalk outside, and Sophie watched the traffic of strangers' feet passing—sneakers and oxfords and a pair of black pumps. She had the sense of being inside an aquarium, the light from the windows casting low, shadowy shapes on the walls, and suggesting strangely that at any time a passerby could stoop down and look in on them. Normally this would have bothered her, made her feel self-conscious and prudish. She was not the sort of girl to make love beneath a bare window. But she was intrigued by herself as Graham imagined her, his vision granting her a certain sense of carelessness that might have been the result of love, or just the thrill of slipping out of herself and becoming someone new. With him, she felt more like the woman she hoped to be—or maybe more like the girl she had once been. She was grateful to him for this, and so she woke him, and kissed him, and enjoyed the possibility that anyone beyond the window might see her there in his bed.

It doesn't matter, she sees now. All romances likely have more to do with vanity than people are willing to admit. It really doesn't matter. One's true nature reveals itself eventually, and there is the real difficulty.

Just last night, after they'd come up to their room from the lounge, and she had washed her face and put on her nightgown, climbed into bed and shut off the light, Graham reached for her beneath the sheet, laid his hand on her belly. "You looked pretty tonight."

"Did I?" She let him kiss her once. His hand was warm through the fabric of her nightgown.

"Beautiful," he said. "You had the table enchanted."

Above their heads, the night reflections of the parking lot lights outside and the blue, aqueous shadows they threw off the surface of the pool played against the ceiling. There were still swimmers, even at this time of night, giggling and splashing, some kind of party happening on the patio, and Sophie felt unlucky suddenly to be here instead of there—in the bed beside Graham and not in the water with the others. She was sorry for herself and for Graham.

"It's late now, and I'm tired," she said. She let out her breath.

When Graham opens his eyes, he realizes he's been sleeping. The skin of his face is tight with sunburn, and he sits up quickly, gathers the blanket, and picks up the lunch sacks that have blown a few feet away into the tangle of ice plant, takes everything back to the car. He assumes Sophie came back and found him asleep, that she will be waiting in the car, silent and irritated and ready to leave. But the car is still locked and empty when he reaches it, and so he dumps the lunch things into the trunk and walks back to the point, lowers himself over the rock where she climbed down an hour before.

The hillside is not so steep as he thought, but there is no trail, and he has to make his way between the woody stalks of some unnameable shrub, step carefully over the ice plant so as not to trip.

From where he walks, he can see nearly the whole of the ocean—the width of the water pushing at the borders of his vision, the borders of the horizon both north and south. Standing here, he can believe in a planet covered in water, everything that is solid and dry subsumed, swallowed up beneath the blue expanse, and he imagines what it would feel like to get into the water, to swim out into the center of it. He tries to picture the shore from that vantage, so distant and small, nothing but a brown stripe of land at the edge of the sky.

At the base of the hillside, the brush turns to gravel and the gravel to rock, and finally Sophie is visible, her figure bent at the side of a tide pool. She has taken off her shoes and rolled up the cuffs of her pants so that her ankles are bare. Her long hair is braided now, the braid hanging over one shoulder.

"We should go," Graham says when he reaches her. He's out of breath from jumping tide pools and hoisting himself over rocks. He's sweating, and his feet feel swollen inside his sandals.

"I'm not finished," Sophie says. "You can go and come back for me if you want." Her palm is cupped around a limpet, its pallid foot suctioned to her skin. There are orange starfish and scuttling red crabs the size of quarters in the pool, anemones whose bristles wave with some unseen tide in the still water.

Graham thinks about the car sitting abandoned at the side of the highway, the dinner back at the hotel that will begin in only another two hours. He'd like to have a shower and a glass of wine or two before they eat.

He stands another moment beside her, shifts his weight.

"Everything is alive here," Sophie says. She edges a fingernail at the body of the limpet, watches it retract slightly into the cone of its shell. "Only I end up cheated."

"Sophie," Graham says now. He cups his hands around hers and lifts the limpet from her palm, then sets it back into the pool, where it retreats again into its shell.

In November, when Sophie had the last miscarriage, a nurse stopped Graham in the hallway of the hospital. "You can't be discouraged," she said. "You deserve a baby."

She was nice, the nurse—middle-aged and soft-faced—and she touched his arm consolingly as she spoke to him, so that Graham could only look at the gloss of the hallway tiles beneath his feet and nod. But when he went into Sophie's room and saw her lying in her hospital bed, what he deserved and what she deserved seemed no longer identifiable. Sophie looked like a stranger to him there—not his bright wife. And this moment not the life he'd been led to expect.

The tide is coming in at their feet, and now and then the spray of a wave hits a rock and splatters Graham's skin and the lenses of his glasses. He removes his glasses, squints out at the water and down the shoreline to where the knobby bodies of the rocks rise gray and misshapen from the water. The bluffs that looked so picturesque from the top of the hillside look scabby here. The water is a little brackish at the edges of the pools, and the white remains of gull-waste spot the rocks.

"The tide," he says as he wipes his glasses on the hem of his shirt and puts them back on.

"Please, just let's sit awhile," Sophie says.

Graham pauses, then sits. "This is where the photos were taken—this line of shore. All of them were taken here. You know which ones I mean—Weston and the rest."

"I recognize it," she says. "It looks different in real life, doesn't it?"

"The photos were probably taken up above." He points to the spot up the hill where he ate.

"I'm not saying they weren't real, just that they don't line up. The photos idolize this place, even if they didn't mean to. They idealize." She is squatting still, her arms wrapped around her calves. "It's a bit of a trick really, this place."

There is wind coming in now with the tide, and it billows the back of her shirt, pulls long strands of her hair from the braid, so that when she raises her face, she looks young and disheveled. If a baby had been born, she might have become a girl who looked like this—a dark-haired girl with Sophie's eyes and long legs.

"I can imagine this place before people," he says. "Prehistory." He looks at her, and she has raised her face to him and is listening. "If you forget about the road up there, you can see this all as it was."

"There would have been more trees. There were probably redwoods leaning right over the bluffs."

"And more fishes," Graham says. "They use words like *teeming* when they talk about the ancient oceans. Oceans *teeming* with fishes."

Sophie nods. "I suppose we're to blame," she says. "Everything was Eden until we came along." It is a joke, even if a small one, and so he smiles.

Graham stands and looks once more at the tide, which fills the tide pools each time a new wave breaks. "Let's go," he says.

They find their way back across the tide pools and the rocks, and then move up the hillside, Graham nervous and his feet sliding on the loose dirt now and then, the smooth soles of his sandals no good for traction. He grasps at handfuls of ice plant to leverage himself, then feels the plant's fingers open up, sticky in his grasp. Behind him, Sophie is quiet, and he glances over his shoulder every few steps to be sure she is following. She climbs easily, taking long strides.

At the car, he opens the trunk and uses the blanket to wipe off his feet. He offers Sophie the rest of the juice, which is warm in the bottle, but she drinks it, anyway.

Graham's camera is in the trunk, an expensive digital camera that he bought for this trip just before leaving home. He's always been a traditionalist, and this camera is something of an embarrassing concession to the time. But, the salesgirl at the photo shop explained, it will automatically crop images or correct a poor use of flash, turn a color photo into a black-and-white if he'd prefer a more classic look. He had thought he would want to take pictures of this coast, at the spots where the best men worked. But he sees now that Sophie was right about the difference between this landscape and the landscape of their photos, and that having first seen their images, he would never be happy with his own. He tucks the camera bag beneath the blanket, shuts the trunk, and gets into the car.

They will drive back to the hotel tonight, and tomorrow will get on a plane and fly east again. And in a few months, he is certain, Sophie will pack her bags and leave him. Now, though, they sit together and watch the light over the ocean just beginning to fade.

In the growing dusk, the water seems to deepen and to expand, navy blue and satined and stretching far too wide to fully see. "Now I can say I've been here," Graham says. And beside him, Sophie smiles. He reaches across the seat and offers her his hand, and she takes it with both of her own, and holds on longer than he expects.

THE DROWNING

AT THE FRONT OF THE ROOM, the boy stood on a carpeted platform and told his drowning story. The girl had drowned in a swimming hole, dove in and hit her head on a rock invisible from the water's surface. Her forehead was bleeding when the two men carried her out of the water. Weeds dangled from her toes; muddy water bubbled from her nostrils and her mouth. And the people on the shore—little kids in their red and yellow trunks and suits, mothers with lunch coolers still in their hands—all stepped away as the men lay her body on the dirt.

The boy made a face as if it was too bad, shook his head. "She acted careless around the water," he said. "Always a big mistake." He looked not much older than Lucy—sixteen or seventeen at the oldest—and wore red shorts, and sandals that slapped at the smooth soles of his feet as he walked back and forth across the small platform. He had recited the story before, Lucy could tell, because he paused in the right places, held his breath when he wanted his listeners to hold theirs.

Lucy sat cross-legged on the carpeted floor of the day camp's borrowed common room and listened. The room was a church sanctuary, the camp itself a Baptist retreat center built on a sprawling plot of donated land in the Santa Monica Mountains. It was a cheap rental, the camp directors had explained to the new counselors, and, with a few alterations, they could make the place look sufficiently less sacred. The folding chairs and the hymnals were removed to a closet, stacked neatly and closed behind accordion doors. The altar was pushed against a far wall, a flowered bedsheet draped over the cross in the corner.

On his stage, the boy gestured now, bending down and scooping up a body of air, and Lucy could see the drowned girl in his arms—just as she was meant to—could imagine him trying to resuscitate her.

The boy was the camp's head lifeguard. He would teach the others assigned to the pool how to keep their eyes on the water at all times, how to sit and scan, he said. He wore a whistle around his neck, and he lifted it to his lips and blew, demonstrating some of the commands, a code the lifeguards would come to understand. "A good lifeguard learns to respect these signals," the boy said, his face serious and stern. "He respects them like he respects the water."

Lucy would not be a lifeguard. She'd been assigned to the Nature Hut, a small manufactured shed on one corner of the camp's grounds. Inside, there were boxes of lessons for her to teach, prepackaged kits she could hand out to the children. *The Sun and Its Power. Gentlemen and Lady Bugs. Forest Detective: Plant ID Spy Kit for Kids.* Lucy had stood in the hot shed earlier in the day, before lunch and the all-camp orientation, and had looked through the boxes. They were stocked with pencils and invisible-ink pen sets, squares of photosensitive paper in small, black plastic bags, plant ID tags, and miniature magnifying glasses. She shuffled through these things, bored, and stuffed them away again, sat down on the dirty floor.

The shed's one window—a high, narrow piece of Plexiglas that did not open—let in only a small, distorted slant of light that wobbled and shifted shape against the wall until Lucy could not look at it anymore and closed her eyes. Above her head, wasps butted their bodies against the Plexiglas in dull thuds. The shed door was open, but they hovered at the window anyway, their wings tremoring against the false glass. Lucy concentrated on their sound, on the way the air in the shed seemed to vibrate with their movement, dizzying her as if the insects were inside her head and swarming. She had sat still until the lunch bell sounded up the hill, then opened her eyes and stepped out of the shed feeling flushed, unsteady on her own two feet.

Now, in the wide cool of the common room, the boy finished his speech by demonstrating some pool commands on his whistle, then bent forward in a clumsy bow, his grin wide. He jumped down from the platform and sat on the carpet again, stretching his legs long, crossing one ankle over the other. For the rest of the afternoon, as the counselors listened to the other presentations, the boy moved his foot so that the plastic sole of the flip-flop slapped quietly against his heel. It was a naked sort of noise that distracted Lucy and kept her aware of the boy's nearness, made him seem to fill the room.

After the meeting, Lucy gathered her purse, unpinned her laminated name tag from her T-shirt, and walked outside. It was a Friday, which meant her father would pick her up. She moved through the crowd of other counselors where they stood on the lawn drinking sodas and eating granola bars, and walked away from their noise, down the dirt drive, toward the road. There was a small ditch along the drive, trenched out over time by the rain that now and then rolled inland off the Pacific with the clouds and smelled like the bottom of the sea. The dirt in the ditch was hard packed and cracking now in the heat, and there were yellowed oak leaves, dried and curled in on one another, lying in clots where the last rain had washed and left them. Lucy fit her feet into the groove of the ditch and walked over the leaves, which sounded like small bones breaking beneath her weight—the frail white bones of a fish, maybe, or the hard-shelled backs of insects.

At the end of the drive, a wrought-iron gate opened onto the paved road, and Lucy stopped and leaned against the gate's frame, let her purse slide down her shoulder to rest on the ground.

"You a lifeguard?" It was the boy in the red shorts. He held a soda in his hand, and pulled a second from his pocket, offering it to her.

Lucy turned around and squinted. "No thank you," she said.

The boy shrugged and dropped the can back into his pocket, and Lucy imagined the soda fizzing, bubbles rising inside the can and against his thigh. "You should think about it," he said.

"I've already been assigned. I'm not a lifeguard."

The boy looked at her, tipped his head back and drank from his soda. His name tag was pinned to the chest of his T-shirt. RAND, it read. She wondered how that could be a name. His name must have been Randal, she thought. Randy. Something common. Something suited to his blond hair and to his face, which was attractive in an expected way—solidly square and jawed, tanned the same color as the dust on his feet. He was the kind of boy who—she knew—would forget what she looked like in a moment, when he turned and left. On Monday she wouldn't be recognizable to him or to any of the red-suit boys, the pack of them lounging high above the pool in their white lifeguard towers, laughing together over the water and the wet heads of counselors and children below.

Lucy squinted into the sunlight again, raised a hand to shade her eyes, then turned her back to the boy. She looked down the long stretch of road for her father. Above her, the sky was flat blue and cloudless. "I'm waiting for my ride," she said. "He'll be here." She hoped the boy might think she was expecting a boyfriend, that he might go and leave her to stand at the gate alone. She could still hear him behind her, though, the shuffling of his flip-flops and the long draw of his breath each time he swallowed a mouthful of his soda.

"This is my third year lifeguarding," he said.

Lucy kept her eyes on the road and folded her arms across her chest.

"No one's ever drowned." He shifted his weight, swallowed. Lucy heard these small movements of his body. She heard the buzzing she'd noticed earlier in the day, at the shed, that same small shiver of sound, and she looked up to locate the source of the hum.

"Bees," the boy said, following her eyes.

"Wasps, actually," Lucy said.

"Bees everywhere this year," the boy told her. "It's a bad year for them. We'll get twenty kids stung—at least." He nodded, lifted his soda can in the direction of the gate head, where a papery gray globe hung inside a wrought-iron curl, swollen and humming with a thin vibration. Several wasps hovered outside the nest, and now and then one darted for its entrance and disappeared inside.

Lucy stared a moment and then crossed the dirt to stand on the other side of the road, across from the gate and the wasps and the boy. There was grass there, growing beneath an oak, and she lowered her purse and sat.

"You won't do so well here if you're afraid of a few bees," the boy said.

He finished his soda, then pulled the other from his pocket and drank it slowly, crumpling the cans between his hands when he had emptied them, leaning against the gate.

In the quiet, Lucy listened to the wasps moving behind the thin shell of their nest above the boy's head. Their sound was strung and frantic, and Lucy thought of them inside, working away at their homemaking and reproduction, building their delicate, papery walls.

The boy looked at his watch. "I don't think he's coming," he said.

"He'll be here," Lucy told him, "so you should just go." She looked at the boy, but he didn't move, and they waited together, not speaking, until her father finally arrived.

On Sunday, Lucy's father woke her late, the sun in the small bedroom window heavy and full with mid-morning. "Wake up, Sleepyhead," he said. He stood over her bed, already dressed, his hair combed and pulled back in a small ponytail at the nape of his neck. Since leaving them, her father had grown his hair to his shoulders and sometimes let it hang long and ungathered in a style that made him look girlish somehow, smaller and effeminate. It curled at the ends, and Lucy thought of the one browning photograph she had seen of her grandfather as an infant—a christening portrait—his body hidden behind several layers of a white lace gown, and his hair in uncut ringlets around his face.

"I suppose he thinks he's goddamn Samson," Lucy's mother had said of her father's hair. But Lucy remained silent, uncertain again where her loyalties should lie.

Now, in the cramped office her father made into a guest bedroom on the weekends, he stooped over her to kiss her forehead as he'd always done, and his hair brushed against her face.

Lucy closed her eyes. The glare from the window was bright, and she motioned for her father to pull the shades.

"I don't think so," he said, turning around to leave. "No, we're up and at 'em this morning, Miss. I let you sleep late as it is." He had taken this tone when speaking to her lately, a tone Lucy knew he meant to sound jovial and bubbly, upbeat. He smiled at her and closed the door, and she could hear him then in the next room, the familiar sound of him turning the pages of the morning newspaper, the silver clanking of his fork against his breakfast plate.

The first weekend she'd stayed with him, she woke up panicked by these sounds, disoriented by the oddity of them. She went to the window, looked down at the white and sprawling body of Los Angeles spread out beyond the apartment, the white shimmer of the ocean in the far distance like an illusion of water on a hot road, and she remembered what had happened. Noise and the absence of noise, Lucy thought. Her mother screaming across the dinner table. Her father slamming doors. So much fighting and then the start of that keening silence that always follows a break.

She rolled out of bed now and pulled on her clothes, stripped the mattress of her sheets and folded them for next time, then heaved the collapsible bed frame back into the couch. Standing with her back to the door, she dressed for the day, stepping out of the pajamas she wore at her father's and throwing them into the hamper, fitting yesterday's underwear into her purse where her father would not see it. She would take them home for her mother to wash later.

In the other room, Lucy dropped her purse on the floor beside her chair and sat for breakfast. Her father had made pancakes, and they lay cold and rubbered on a plate in the center of his small table. He nudged them toward her. "You can nuke them," he said.

Lucy sensed him watching as she forked a pancake onto her plate, poured the syrup and capped it. When she cut and ate her first bite, he smiled congenially, satisfied, opened the newspaper again and disappeared behind a page of black-and-white advertisements for kitchen appliances and lingerie and home decor.

"I have a fun day planned for us," he said from behind the newsprint as Lucy chewed her cold breakfast. "A really fun day."

* * *

Midway through the first week of camp, Lucy took her lunch to the pool. She'd packed her swimsuit into her purse in the morning and stood in line behind a row of children at the bathhouse, waiting for a stall in which to change. She ate as she waited, picking at the sandwich her mother had made, throwing the rest into the trash inside the bathroom before closing herself into the far stall. The bathroom was dark and wet, and the voices of little girls bounced off the cinder-block walls as she took off her clothes and pulled on the swimsuit. Her suit was a black one-piece from the women's department, selected to hide the bit of weight she'd gained since last summer. It had darts down the front that her mother said would camouflage her tummy, and large matronly bra cups the color of milk.

At the cloudy mirror beyond the stalls, Lucy leaned in to look at her face, pinching color into her plain cheeks with her fingertips, working her brown hair into a braid. She turned her backside toward the reflection and looked at the pale shapes of her legs in the mirror, the unfamiliar, fleshy round of her own hip, then reached again into her purse for her shorts, tugged them on before walking out into the white noon sun.

Outside, the pool gate was locked, and Lucy motioned for one of the other counselors to let her in. The pool was closed to children during the lunch hour, though a few of them still stood around the perimeter with their lunch bags, leaning their backs against the chain-link fence, hoping to be the first ones into the water after the break. Around the pool, there were only a handful of counselors sunning themselves, their towels spread and their sodas and magazines and tanning lotions set out beside them.

Lucy found a towel in the clean stack kept near the gate and unrolled it on the pavement, slid off her shoes and sat. The water was an aqua sheet, smooth and unmoved by any breeze. Light glazed its surface, and when she lay back on her towel, hand raised above her eyes, Lucy saw the reflection the water created on the base of the diving board, a tight honeycomb of light that seemed to expand and constrict, expand and constrict.

"You here to swim?" the boy asked. He had crouched down beside her, too close, and she thought she could hear the fizz in his soda can again.

"I don't swim," Lucy said. She closed her eyes and felt the sun on her face, hot and silver-tinted behind her eyelids. She'd thought about the boy since last seeing him, had imagined him leaning over the body of the girl in his story, his mouth against hers, open and breathing. The thought flushed Lucy's face now.

"It's warm out today," the boy said. "You should get in. You're down in that dust pit at Nature. Get in and wash the dirt off."

Someone else had climbed into the pool, and there was the quiet sound of a body moving through the water, the lapping of waves against the tile lip of the pool.

On the weekend, with her father, Lucy had put her feet into the Pacific. She'd walked beside him, her arms outstretched and her fingers extended wide and straight as a child's might be, tensed with the chill of the water, with the closeness of her father. Once the water level reached her father's waist, he dunked down and began to swim, his head and arms barely visible. "Come on," he hollered. Lucy didn't, though. She stood and watched his dark figure move out farther and farther. When he finally turned back toward her, his face had become featureless with distance, the sunlight obscuring Lucy's view of him, obscuring the line she'd imagined running between the two of them across the water's choppy surface.

At the pool, the boy stepped out of his flip-flops. "Come on," he said again. "I'll swim with you." He moved to the edge of the pool and stood waiting for her, rising up and down, up and down on the balls of his bare feet, flexing the muscles of his calves.

Lucy sat up and began rolling her towel. She pulled her shirt from her purse and slid it on over her head. "I don't swim," she said again.

The boy looked at her. "Afraid of bees *and* drowning?" he said. "You really know how to live." He grinned, and the light caught the whistle at his chest, flashed so that Lucy winced as she stood. She let herself out through the gate and walked off down the hill in the heat.

Friday afternoon, it was Lucy's mother who arrived after camp. "Your father couldn't make room in his busy bachelor's schedule to get you today," she said when Lucy opened the car's passenger door. "I'm driving you to his place." All the way into the city, her mother kept the radio loud and tuned to a talk station, the angry voices of callers and hosts knitting together in the tight space of the car. When they reached the freeway traffic, her mother rolled down the window, lit a cigarette, and began to smoke.

"I wish you wouldn't," Lucy said. She folded her arms over her body, her head pressed against the glass of her window, and she looked to her mother, who had dressed for this drive. She'd put on lipstick and the big Jackie Kennedy sunglasses she said were chic. She'd clipped on a pair of silver earrings that dangled in teardrops from her ears and sparkled with the light as she turned her head to exhale a breath of smoke out the window.

"We only get so many wishes in life, Lucy," her mother said. "I wouldn't go throwing mine away at such a young age."

At the corner near her father's building, her mother stopped, and Lucy got out and closed the car door. The window slid down, and her mother leaned toward her, the sunglasses wide across her cheekbones, hiding her face, the cigarette still burning between her fingers. She lowered the volume on the radio. "Lu," she said. "If your father asks about me—" Her voice was tired and tense.

"Don't," Lucy said. She'd turned her back on her mother and walked down the block to the building's entrance, rode the elevator to her father's floor.

Her father was late, and she waited for him, paging through the magazines he kept on the coffee table. When she heard his keys at the front door, and he finally appeared, he was dressed not in his workday uniform of trousers and white shirt, but in Bermuda shorts and sandals, his long hair tucked behind his ears and held back by the sunglasses he had pushed up on his head like a headband. Lucy put down her magazine and got up to cross the room toward him. They stood a moment, and then he leaned forward and hugged her, quickly, too tight. "Glad you're here, kid. Really glad you're here."

"I was early, maybe," she said. "I've been waiting awhile."

"No, no. My fault." He stepped away from her and into the kitchen, pulled two cans of soda from his undersized refrigerator. Lucy had wondered about the refrigerator when he'd first moved into the apartment. It was meant for a room in a dormitory or a motel. It could hold a pint of milk, a loaf of bread, a six-pack of soda or beer. She wondered how her father ate when she was with her mother, if he cooked for himself now that no one was cooking for him. She pictured him moving down the lit aisles of the IGA at midnight, one of those plastic baskets in his hands, and inside it, a frozen pizza, one can of green beans, one prepackaged brownie. She imagined him winking at the cashier as his purchases were rung up, saying, "Life of the single guy, eh?" The thought took her breath.

Her father sat on the couch beside her, close, so that she had to shift slightly away, and he opened both sodas and handed her one, smiled. Later they'd be going out to dinner on the Pier, he said, and then to a movie, and then ice cream if she was good. He winked. Tomorrow there'd be golfing at the course near his apartment, and time by the apartment pool, an hour for resting before burgers and shakes and a walk through Third Street to watch the jugglers and mimes and tarot card readers before dark. Her father told her this, and then he was quiet, folding one leg over the other the way he always had, but awkward now and stiff. "What do you think of that, kid?" he asked.

"Great," Lucy said.

They sat beside each other drinking their sodas, the apartment silent except for the tiny vibrations of the refrigerator in the kitchen, the white thrum of rush-hour traffic beyond the window as so many people headed home.

When Lucy arrived at camp the next Friday morning, the sky was low, the air thick and wet and suffocating. She moved through her morning slowly, slipping into the shed between classes to reach up under her T-shirt, unstick the fabric from her skin, and wipe away the line of sweat that had gathered beneath her bra. All afternoon the children complained of the heat. "Take us to the pool," one little girl demanded, throwing her project into the dirt at her feet. Lucy had given each child photographic paper, for sun prints, but the images came out pale instead of deep blue, the white shapes of the leaves and rocks and twigs they'd tried to imprint indistinct and disappointing.

"You've all had swim time already today," Lucy said. She ignored the girl's whining but looked up the hill in the direction of the pool, thought of slipping just her feet into the water, feeling the cool climb all the way up her legs.

At the end of the day, Lucy collected her purse and walked to the gate to wait for her father. The heat still throbbed around her, and the sky burned a hard white, bright enough that Lucy sat and put her hands to her face, closed her eyes behind them. She was there when she heard the boy walk toward her.

"What are you afraid of now?" he asked, his red shorts still wet from the pool.

Lucy didn't stand.

"You waiting for your ride again?" He nodded his head in the direction of the staff parking lot. "I got my car. I'll take you home if you tell me where." His shorts dripped water that fell and beaded on the dust at his feet. "Or we can go somewhere." His voice pitched with the idea, and he grinned. "I know a place I bet you haven't seen."

Lucy looked away from him. "I'll wait," she said. She pulled her purse onto her lap, holding it close to her chest. She could smell chlorine on the boy's body, the strong chemical blue scent of the pool still on his skin, on his suit and in his hair. Her own hair was no doubt a mess, her skin sweet with the stink of sweating all day.

The boy didn't move. "No, come on," he said.

Lucy followed him across camp. The hill to the parking lot was steep and graveled, and the boy held his hand out to her, taking her arm himself when she ignored the offer. When they reached his car, he opened the passenger door first, and Lucy got in.

The car was overheated after sitting in the sun all day, and it smelled of Boy—damp and musky, like socks and aftershave and the earthy, green smell of grass. A faded cardboard air freshener swung from the rearview, scentless.

"I know a place," the boy said. He climbed into his seat beside her, put his hand on her thigh. Through her shorts, Lucy could feel all five of his fingers, and she straightened, felt her face warm.

"Let's just go," she said.

The boy reached forward as he drove and turned on the radio, raising the volume, moving between stations before settling on one and sitting back. "You've probably never been to this place. It's one of those things, you know . . ." He looked at her. "One of those spots that's just great but that nobody knows about." The boy smiled, turned up the volume on the radio again, and drummed his thumbs along the steering wheel.

Lucy looked at him. "I'll need to be back," she said. Her voice was small against the music, and she tried to shout. "I can go for a few minutes, but I need to get back to the camp." She tucked her hands into a tight clasp in her lap, hugged her purse as the boy turned onto the highway. "My father is just a little late," she yelled. "He'll be waiting for me."

The boy nodded his head to the stiff beat of the music, merged the car onto the freeway.

Lucy thought about her father as they drove. Her father had rolled down all of the windows on their way home from the beach last weekend. He had opened the sunroof and taken his hands from the wheel, raising them up to the wind and the sky as the car moved undirected down the highway. "Isn't this great, Lucy!" he shouted. Beside them, the Pacific moved, swift and black and boundaryless. "Isn't this living, Lu?" her father had laughed.

In the car, the boy pulled off the freeway onto a local road. "Are you sure you know where you're going?" Lucy asked. They had left the familiar suburban landscape of strip malls and tile-roofed housing developments behind them, and now all that stood along the sides of the road were trees.

The boy rounded a corner and the tires stuttered onto a dirt road. "Of course I know," he said. Dust rose around the car in gray-brown plumes until the boy slowed, and Lucy could see that the road dead-ended in a parking lot. "We're here," the boy said. He seemed pleased. He parked and got out, then moved around the car to let Lucy out, holding her hand again. "We're here, but we still have to walk a ways."

He led her down a narrow path. Above their heads, oaks and eucalyptus trees made a deep shade, the trees' dark leaves knitting together so that only fragments of sunlight were visible. Lucy could smell the ocean drifting in from over the brown backs of the hills.

"I don't know this place," she said. "I don't know where I am."
But the boy took it as a compliment, and he turned to look at her,
squeezed her hand in his.

Where the path began to descend, he let go of her hand, and the
two of them scrambled down over rocks toward a grove of oaks that
opened onto a swimming hole.

"This is it," the boy said. He stretched his arms out wide. "It's a
sort of canyon. I'll bet there was a river here once."

The water was still now, not a river, but a pool, deep and glassy
and nearly black. When she stood near its edge, Lucy could see the
tendrils of grasses and weeds reaching up toward the surface and the
light, though at this time of day the water was shadowed by the rock
walls that stood around the pool, fencing it. The rock was knobbed
and pocked and uneven with erosion, and there were narrow ledges
and outcroppings here and there, deep notches the size of fingers
or fists. Tufts of blond grass grew from between the rock's cracks, and
where there were larger splits, yellowing bushes and skinny oaks
pressed together, tangled and scrawny, apparently unrooted.

"I thought we could swim," the boy said. He dropped her hand
and stripped off his shirt and flip-flops, started out around the perimeter of the water, and climbed up onto a ledge of rock at the far
side, where he began to inch away from Lucy. She watched him and
the reflection of him on the water a few feet below. The reflection
wobbled and shimmied, fracturing and reassembling with the motion
of the water.

"I should get back," Lucy said. She said it once, quietly, then
again louder, raising her voice so that it carried down the small canyon
in an echo.

"You just swim if you fall." The boy did not look back to her.
He moved carefully, stopping to readjust his balance, then stepping
forward again, his feet awkward beneath him.

"You should come down from there," Lucy said. She stood still. She thought about the story—the boy's story. The drowned girl and the rocks. The water and the way the girl had come up gurgling it from her dead mouth like breath. She wondered about the truth of the story; wondered if the boy had created it, a fiction to frighten his audience, to make himself somehow the hero.

In a moment, the boy moved out of her vision, behind two large boulders that humped into the water at the far end of the pool. Lucy kept her eyes on the rocks where he had last been, but then he appeared at the top of one of the boulders. He arched forward and dove, his body sending rings across the surface of the water that grew wider and wider until they broke against the shore where Lucy stood. She stepped back.

Lucy had not swum since childhood. When she was a little girl, her parents had taken her on summer afternoons to the city pool. It was crowded and loud, the water always busy with so many arms and flailing legs, and the scent of chlorine heavy and chemical, rising off the pool like a haze. Lucy's parents spread their towels on the concrete deck near the chain-link fence that surrounded the pool and sat back to watch. "Get in," her mother would say from her spot against the fence. "Go on and play with the others." She made shooing motions with her hand, frowned from beneath the wide brim of her straw hat, as if Lucy were disappointing her, being a baby.

If Lucy stood long enough, however, her father would get up and walk around the pool to the deep end, climb the ladder to the high dive and stand at the top, waving to her a moment before diving in. He always stood very straight, the end of the long board bouncing slightly with the weight of his body, so that he seemed precarious there, so far up, and tiny. He flapped his arms like wings, clowning, then bent forward and jumped in. There would be years, it seemed to Lucy, before he surfaced, suddenly and unexpected, always right beside her in the shallow end.

Only once had he talked her into jumping, and that was from the low board. "I'll be here," he said, pointing to the spot where he stood in the shallow end. "Swim to me. I'll be here when you come up." Lucy came up sputtering in the deep end, though, disoriented, her eyes stinging and her vision blurry, her nose burning with the gulp she'd inhaled, and her ears ringing. She moved her legs beneath her, treading water there in the middle of the pool, waiting, then finally swam for the nearest edge and climbed out, crossed the concrete to her mother, who handed her a towel, said, "Well, I guess you won't be foolish enough to do that again, will you?"

Now Lucy took another step away from the water and looked for the boy at the center of the swimming hole until he surfaced, blowing air from his mouth as he rose, reaching up to wipe his eyes and smooth back his hair. He swam to where the water shallowed and walked to the shore, gathered his shirt and shoes in a wad under his arm.

When he reached Lucy, he put his hand on her shoulder. "Look," he said. He pointed to an oak branch that leaned out over the water, above their heads.

Lucy looked up. Her shirtsleeve was wet where he had touched her. "What?" she said. "What am I supposed to see?" Between the leaves she could just make out the gray shape of a wasps' nest, fatter than the one she had seen at camp, perfect, the size of a fist, maybe, or of a heart.

At her side, the boy pushed his foot through the dirt, then stooped to pick up a rock he had uncovered. He closed one eye and pitched back. The rock left his hand. "Run!" the boy hollered, and he took off laughing toward the trail back to the car.

On the shore, Lucy didn't run. She had seen the rock pass, awful, through the gray sphere of the wasps' nest, breaking it the way she imagined a piñata might break, the fragile paper shell tearing and a confetti of insects falling, stunned and angry, into the open air. They seemed to hover there now, their yellow bodies glinting like flecks of fool's gold in the sun, and she knew in an instant they would search out any live thing and sting.

Lucy dropped her purse to the ground and slid off her shoes, stepped out into the water to her ankles, her calves, her waist. Below her, the grasses moved against her legs and the ground disappeared. She imagined the wasps as she dipped her head beneath the surface— their frantic buzzing like the buzzing of the water rushing into her ears, their movements disoriented and unsteady where they shivered above the broken husk of their nest. They would have to rebuild, she thought as she let the water close in around her. Start over.

When she could not hold her breath any longer, Lucy bubbled to the surface. In her head, there was still a quiet hum and a dizziness as her feet felt the absence of anything solid beneath them, as her body moved weightless toward the open air.

THE BATH

THIS IS MY MOTHER. She is wearing her camel coat and beneath it her white uniform. It is a cold afternoon to be wearing a cotton uniform, and the wind is fierce coming off Lake Michigan, fierce blowing between the old brick apartment buildings and through the bare branches of the oak and cherry trees that stand along the street. Lately, it has occurred to my mother that this wind—this chill in the air and the snow it brings nightly—is perhaps a permanent season. The cold will outlast winter and run into May and June, and the trees will remain as they are now—wrought iron and skeletal against a white January sky. She reaches up to pinch closed the collar of her coat and moves slowly down the sidewalk, her feet invisible to her beneath the mound of her belly, in which I am waiting to be born.

At the corner, my mother enters the last building on the block and pauses in the lobby for the elevator. The building is as old as the others, but it is meant to look modern inside, the brick walls plastered over and textured, and the ceiling sparkling with flecks of false gold in the low light of a chandelier. There are potted silk palms, and on the walls, framed prints featuring abstract slashes of paint in colors like avocado and deep orange and wheat. The carpet is thick and also gold, and its bunched nap gives a little beneath my mother's white shoes as she shifts her weight from foot to foot and listens to the elevator chiming its descent.

The apartment my mother shares with my father is on the other side of the hospital, nearer the university where my father studies, in the sort of neighborhood people might say to avoid. When they first moved to the city, they rented a flat from a professor—the basement of a Tudor-style house on a street of wide brick Colonials and a short string of upright and tidy brownstones. It was a street of lawns and driveways, of potted geraniums and narrow, pleached walks that wrapped around the houses toward backyard gardens. But the basement was small, and my mother found the smell of mildew in her socks after walking on the carpet, found the pink scent of mold in her towels, and saw flushed colonies of it spreading up the plastic sheet of the shower curtain and blooming quietly on the wall behind the bed. These things she could tolerate, but the professor said a baby would be trouble, and so my parents moved in my mother's fifth month, before I could disrupt the household.

The apartment they moved to was larger in some ways, smaller in others. It had higher ceilings, and a clean but tiny bathroom, and windows that let in light that glinted against the linoleum floors of the kitchen and living room. It had counter space, and heavy cast-iron radiators, and a narrow but mold-less tiled shower. It would be, my parents decided, sufficient.

Now, in this finer apartment lobby, the elevator arrives, and my mother gets in and rides to the tenth floor. Min is waiting when the doors slide open, and she smiles at my mother, holds out one of her small hands. "Hello," she says. She has changed out of her nurse's uniform and has put on a pale sweater set, beige slacks, a pair of red embroidered satin slippers. She wears a neat string of pearls around her neck.

"You look so fancy," my mother says. "Maybe you have a date later? It was kind of you to invite me. I won't keep you long."

"No," Min says. She seems to blush. "No. I am so glad to have you come."

My mother is still catching her breath from the walk in the wind. Her hands are cold when she puts them back in her pockets and follows Min down the hallway to her door. Once inside, in the sudden heat of the apartment, she feels that her face is cold as well, flushed with the outdoor chill. She touches the backs of her hands to her cheeks, then takes off her coat and hands it to Min. "I'm afraid I'm in my uniform still," she says. "No time to change."

Min frowns at this, but turns and disappears with the coat into another room for a moment before returning with the tea. A tray on the coffee table holds a teapot and two cups and two saucers, and a platter of cut, raw vegetables. "Sit," Min says to my mother, and nods toward the table and the sofa and armchair positioned around it. "Please, sit and be at home."

My mother watches as Min pours amber-colored tea into the china cups. The cups are fragile looking—white porcelain with gold rims—and the pot is part of the set, its belly painted in tiny gold stars and foreign lettering to match. "Loose leaf," Min says. "It is better." Min does not offer milk or sugar, but replaces the cup on its saucer, hands it to my mother, and takes up her own, then sits perched on the edge of her white sofa.

Min is older than my mother by more than a decade, though her face is still young and beautiful. She keeps her black hair trimmed blunt across her forehead and bobbed, a cut that makes her eyes seem large and doll-like, and gives her the look of a woman in her late twenties rather than her early forties.

"This is good," my mother says after her first sip of tea. "I'm used to so much sugar, I guess. But this way is good, too. You really taste the tea this way, don't you?" She feels she is saying more than she should, but across the table Min is so quiet. "It's very good," she says again. "Very hot. No sugar must be the key to that trim figure of yours." My mother laughs, and Min smiles widely and nods. She has not gained even half a pound since she first came to this country from Korea, she explains.

"It is all about one's diet," she says, her face wide and beaming. She lifts the lid off the teapot to pour herself another cup. "Tea and vegetables. This is the secret." Min moves her hand over the tray the way a game-show hostess might, as if revealing something wonderful. On the platter she has neatly stacked a pyramid of chopped celery stalks, a row of narrow carrot sticks, and two pieces of crustless white bread spread thickly with margarine and cut on the diagonal. This is her one weakness, she confesses: Wonder Bread. She allows herself one slice a day. "I do my exercise, too," she says. "I run, but only here, in my apartment. I run for one hour every night before bed, inside, where it is safe and there is never snow." She laughs—a quick, giddy laugh, as if she has perhaps revealed too much about herself—and raises her tea like a toast before sipping it.

My mother imagines Min in her pajamas, her small body darting about between the large white armchairs and the sofa, circling the dining table and rounding the room behind the brass floor lamps. She tries not to smile.

At work, Min arrives looking starched and polished, her white uniform pants creased with the recent press of her iron, her white shoes buffed and their soles soundless on the tiled floor of the hospital corridor as she moves. She still wears a cap, though most of the younger nurses have recently given theirs up. "Should doctors abandon lab coats?" Min asks in the nurses' lounge. The younger women laugh. "Should stewardesses wear Levi Strauss?" She pins her cap to her hair with black bobby pins, where it sits straight on the crown of her head all day as she bends to attend to bedpans and set IVs.

My mother and Min sit together chewing celery and carrots without speaking for another few moments, then Min turns to my mother, replacing her teacup and saucer on the enamel tray. "You may use the bath whenever you are ready," she says. She folds her hands on her knees, and so my mother sets her tea on the tray and stands, smoothing out the fronts of her slacks, which are stained with a rusty splatter of iodine, and wrinkled from her day at the hospital.

Min nods. "There is a towel prepared for you, but no robe. You are much too big for my robe." She laughs beneath her hand as if she has said something very funny, and points my mother down the hallway.

In the bathroom, my mother goes to the tub, turns on the hot water, and undresses, folding her clothes. Her maternity underwear is large and beige, and she balls and tucks it into the front pocket of her uniform shirt, then places the stack of clothes on top of the plush toilet-seat cover. The room is three times the size of her bathroom at home and is all white. The walls are papered in a white-and-ivory-stripe pattern; the countertop is white laminate, strung through with thin ribbons of gold; the bath mat and throw rugs are like the thick coat of a white dog. To my mother's back there is a wide mirror that runs the whole length of the wall above the sink and is rimmed in vanity lights that reflect off the surface of the water filling the tub. My mother turns and looks at herself. Her mirror at home is narrow, only good for seeing that one's pants match one's shirt, that one's lipstick is not crooked. This mirror, however, is perfect. In it, her belly is round and tight, the skin around her navel and across her breasts stretched and so shiny she seems nearly silvered, like something amphibian, legs and arms of a mammal but the polished, bloated body of a fish.

In the nurses' lounge at work she told Min that she wasn't certain she recognized herself anymore. She said it as if she were telling a joke, smiling, waiting for Min to smile, too. "It's as if I've put on someone else's skin," my mother said. "I've lost all control over my own proportions."

Min's face was pinched and serious. "You should find water," she said. "Get into a pool or a deep bath. I have a deep bath. When I'm in it, I float. I forget my body." For a moment both women were quiet, and Min stood then, collected her lunch, folding the empty plastic bags and capping her thermos, burying everything inside her purse. It was not until later, in the hallway, that she stopped my mother, invited her to come and use the tub.

Now my mother is staring at herself in the clouding mirror when Min raps at the door. "You are enjoying the water?" Min asks from the other side.

"Yes," my mother calls, her voice sounding startled, as if she has been caught at something illicit. She shuts off the tap and climbs quickly into the hot water.

Beyond the door there is a pause, and then the nearly silent pad of Min's feet as she makes her way back out to the other room.

My mother crosses her arms, covering her chest, but then eases. My father would find it strange that she accepted Min's offer—that she is here in another woman's tub, nude and so ungainly. She slips down and puts him out of her mind, though, displacing water so that a bit spills over the lip of the tub to the white rug below.

By the time my father arrives home from his classes, it is dark outside and my mother has dinner in the oven. When he steps through the door, she sees him lift his nose slightly, smelling the onions and garlic of the casserole she has made. He takes off his coat and hangs it on the rack by the door, where beads of melted snow run down the nylon and fall in drips to the linoleum floor. When he comes home in the evening, his face is always flushed from the walk in the cold, and his long hair has been blown back from his forehead by the wind. He has been growing his hair only since starting graduate school, but it hangs nearly to his shoulders now and is wavy. The hair is meant to look intellectual and a little rebellious, meant to match the secondhand corduroy blazer with its patches on the elbows, its worn collar and cuffs. But on him the long hair looks boyish and adolescent, giving him the appearance of a high-school student rather than a grown man.

My mother looks at him and puts her hands to her belly. "Good day today?" she asks.

He crosses the room to where she sits at the table with a magazine, leans forward and kisses her cheek. "My day was fine."

He smells of the city—the wet, dirty smell of the sidewalks and the bodily smell of the bus. She rode the bus today as well, from Min's apartment, and when she arrived home and took off her uniform, she could smell on her clothes the woolen, sweaty scent she always notices on the bus, the overindulgent perfume of Min's shampoo in her hair. She got into the cramped shower of her own bathroom and rinsed off again, then pulled on new underwear, a clean T-shirt, and sweater and pants.

My father straightens from their kiss, and his hair brushes her face. He steps into the kitchen and begins pulling plates and glasses from the cupboards to set the table for dinner.

"I'll do that," she says. She braces against the arms of her chair, pushes herself up.

"You should sit," my father says. "Just sit down." He moves around the little table, setting his side first, laying out the spoon and knife against the place mat, then steps around the high chair they have already bought to set hers. She lifts the magazine and pushes back in her chair to give him room.

They have become this way since the pregnancy—mannered around each other, modest. At night, after my mother rises from the couch and turns off the television, she goes into the bedroom and shuts the door. She pulls her nightgown over her head in the darkness of the bedroom, then, once she is no longer naked, opens the door again, calls into the front room that she is going to bed.

He has adjusted to these changes in her and seems to respect them, stepping around her when they meet in the narrow hallway, turning his back to her when he climbs into bed.

Once, on the night of a dinner with some friends, he walked in on her standing in front of the open closet, deciding what to wear. She was in only her stockings, the waist of the nylons stretched wide, so that the shiny scales of elastic grain were visible around her large middle, her legs iridescent behind the material and her breasts above the waistband heavy and bare. She stood still a moment, then crossed the room to him, touched his chest. "Get out," she said.

He looked at her, put his hand to her shoulder. "This is our room."

"No," she said, and shifted away from him, crossing her arms over her chest. "I need you to go. Please."

He stood with his hand on the doorknob, then stepped back and closed the bedroom door.

At the dining table, my father excuses himself when he leans over her plate to settle the fork on her napkin. He goes to the kitchen for the casserole and brings it to the table, where they eat together beside the window, looking out through the reflection of themselves to the high, stripped branches of the oak trees and the bright windows of their neighbors' apartments.

In the middle of the night, again unable to sleep, my mother gets up and stands at this window with her hands open over the radiator, waiting for the heat to rise. She looks out to wet streets and the walls of other apartments, and notices the pressing sense of the buildings closing in on one another in a way she had not paid attention to before visiting Min's tidier block. My mother imagines the apartment buildings in cross section, the front walls cut away and the interiors revealed. She sits down in the secondhand rocking chair my father bought for her and moves her feet back and forth across the cold linoleum, rocking, rubbing circles on the surface of her belly. She closes her eyes and pictures the apartments stacked like dollhouse rooms— a family tucked into their beds; a young man awake and eating ice cream in front of the blue glare of a television set; an old woman on the seventh floor taking out her teeth and rolling her hair around pink sponge rollers. My mother feels about the closeness of her neighbors as she has come to feel about so many things lately—people's breath against her neck on the bus, her patients' well-meaning hugs, the press of my father's back to hers as they lie in bed at night, and, even though she does not wish to admit it, the clutter of my movements within her. These familiarities are intrusions, unwelcome and embarrassing intimacies with near strangers.

Min begins to invite my mother over once a week to use the tub. At work, these visits go unmentioned, and Min's behavior toward my mother does not change—her nods when they pass each other in the hallway are as curt as ever, her conversations clipped and professional. After work, however, at her apartment, she opens the door warmly, seats my mother on her couch, and serves her tea on a tray. "I'm glad you've come," she always says. "I'm glad to have your company."

Min's apartment has a cool, stark quality that my mother likes, a sense of order and calm that removes the apartment from the building and the city and makes it seem a sort of island. The two women sit on the white cushions of Min's couch and Min talks eagerly for a few moments about a subject it seems she has selected for the day and rehearsed. She holds her teacup between her two hands, and her mouth moves around the words with precision as she speaks them, each syllable exact.

Min tells my mother that when she came to this country she listened to the radio even as she slept, in an effort to ingrain the English language in her mind. All night, as she lay in her bed, the sounds of American pop songs and late-night DJs sifted into and out of her dreams, the idea being that the English syllables would settle as she slept, lodging themselves somewhere deep against the root of her Korean tongue. "It did not work," she confesses. "The words were strangers to me; I did not know them." She bends forward, places her cup onto its saucer, and laces her fingers together over her knees. "And then I did not know Korean anymore, either," she says. "I lost familiarity. The words in my own head might have been someone else's." She raises her shoulders in a shrug, lets out a breath like a sigh. "It doesn't matter," she says. "I made my choice when I moved here. I won't go back to Korea, anyway."

My mother asks about Korea, and Min seems to tighten inside her pink sweater. "Oh, you don't want to know about that," she says.

My mother has heard rumors at the hospital that Min ran from a vicious father or a violent husband. That she was betrothed there, in her village; that she was shamed somehow, and so unmarriageable. All of these scenarios seem impossible. My mother tries to imagine Min as someone's wife, a child twined to Min's body with wide swaths of cloth, the way she has seen women carrying their children in the glossy spreads of *National Geographic*. Those women are always bent with the weight of something—an oversized basket of rice or a jug of water balanced precariously on their heads, the body of another, older child wrapped around them and clinging piggyback as they go about their chores. My mother cannot see Min burdened that way.

At work, Min moves with a frenetic efficiency, her nimble fingers working over a set of stitches or setting an IV needle with trim speed, her white-stockinged legs scissoring down the hallway as she makes her midday rounds. My mother has watched Min work, and she is envious of her straight carriage, her upright and unaccented way of speaking, as if she is in full possession of herself at all times.

My mother looks to Min. "Good you didn't stay in Korea," she says. "You would have likely ended up a housewife. You would have had this." She laughs and arches her back a bit, pats the protrusion of her stomach.

Min sits forward on the couch, picks up her teacup and sips from it, then sets it down again without rattling the china. "When I was first here," she says, and she sweeps her hand out in a gesture at the apartment, "a man came in while I was gone and burgled me. He took only a few things—a piece of jewelry, a radio. I think he took some of my clothes, too." Min wrinkles her nose at this. "He was gone when I arrived home again, but his boot tracks were on my carpet." She points at the blank, white rug near the front door and my mother follows her finger.

"That's horrible," my mother says. "You must have been so upset."

"Yes," Min says simply, "I was."

"You know," my mother says, perhaps too intimately, "sometimes my own husband seems like a strange man to me. I know everything about him," she says, leaning forward on the couch, so that Min pulls back. "I know his peculiarities, his habits. I know him, and still sometimes I see him out of the corner of my eye, and I don't quite recognize him." She crosses her arms over the awkward bulk of her middle. "And then there's the baby." She sets her teacup on its saucer, so that the tea she has not finished sloshes but does not spill. "I shouldn't think these things, but I do."

There is a long moment in which Min does not respond to this confession, and my mother feels the prickly heat of shame climb her chest beneath her blouse.

Min stands. "I see it is dark outside," she says. "Your bath will chill." She stoops to collect the teacups and the tray, and makes her way toward the kitchen as my mother gathers her sweater from the couch and pushes herself to standing.

At the doorway, Min stops. "Each person has his own burden," she says, and she steps out of sight into the kitchen, the teacups clattering slightly on their saucers.

Later, lying beside my father as he sleeps, my mother considers Min's words as she listens to his breathing. His breathing is easy and regular, and she watches his stomach rise and fall, watches the patterns of light kaleidoscoping on the ceiling above her head as cars pass in the street beneath the window. When she met my father, my mother was just out of high school and sitting on the ledge of her open college dorm room window. My father was standing on the grass below. In the story I will hear my father tell later over dinner tables and at backyard barbecues, she called down to him, told him she was thinking of jumping if he didn't come up and pull her back inside. "I stood back," he will joke. "I told her I'd always hoped I'd meet a woman who could surprise me."

This is his memory of their meeting, however, and in my mother's he was the one who called to her first, yelling up a warning not to fall from her perch in the fourth-floor window, where she sat with her legs flung over the ledge into the sun. From her vantage, my father looked small and studious, with his books tucked up under his arm and his small glasses reflecting a glare so that she could not see his eyes. "He looked," she'll say, reaching her own punch line, "so harmless."

* * *

A couple of weeks pass, and my mother does not walk to Min's for her bath. She finds herself thinking about Min's apartment, though—the white armchairs and the silence, the solitude of Min's after-work life. In empty moments, she recalls the buoyant relief of her body submerged beneath the water in that tub.

"Where's your mind off to?" my father asks one evening over dinner. He has been talking and she has missed it.

"Daydreaming, I guess," she says.

"Why don't you tell me?" He lifts his milk glass to his mouth and drinks, then touches his napkin to his lips. In the bright light of the lamp that hangs above the table, the rounds of his eyeglasses are two opaque circles. He reaches across the table to touch her hand.

"Just about the baby," my mother says, sliding her fingers from beneath his grasp. "And how much there is still to do."

"You shouldn't worry about it. You worry too much. Everything will fall together in time." He smiles, and she can see his earnestness, the sincerity with which he hopes her worries, her stress—whatever it is that they both see has shifted in her—will dissipate. He seems young and in need of her.

"You're right," she says. "I'm sure it will."

The next Monday, when my mother ends her shift and walks to the nurses' lounge, Min is there. Min nods at my mother but doesn't turn from where she stands in front of her locker, and so my mother crosses the room toward her, apologizes for not stopping by in so long. "I've been busy," my mother lies. "But today I'm free. Today would be a good day for tea," she says. And then she invites Min to come home with her this afternoon instead. "I should make the tea this time," she says. "You should let me make the tea."

Min stops buttoning her red coat for a moment and stares down at her feet.

"It's not as nice as yours," my mother says. "My place, I mean. It's shabby, really. But I've been meaning to thank you for your hospitality."

There is another woman in the lounge, an older nurse, someone Min's age, and Min turns to see if she has heard, but the woman has her magazine opened and does not look up.

"That's fine." Min nods then, her voice low, and she works the buttons on her coat, pulls on a pale and fuzzy hat, and walks beside my mother out of the building.

Outside, the snow on the hospital lawn has begun to melt, and patches of grass show through brown and muddy and thin. The buildings of the university rise up across the street, their stone-block walls high and the greening copper roofs slacking snow in great icy sheets in the afternoon warmth. Walking with Min, my mother looks down at the sidewalk and watches the way the soft prints her shoes press into the slush disappear quickly behind her, the way the cloud of her breath evaporates in the warming March air. She turns to Min, who has tucked her face into the high collar of her coat against the wind and has buried her hands in her pockets. "You too cold?" my mother asks.

"I'm fine," Min says. She does not look up but moves in a trudge at my mother's side until they reach the apartment.

My mother unlocks the lobby door and pushes it open. There are three vinyl chairs seated around a kidney-bean-shaped table, copies of expired entertainment magazines and the *News Tribune* lying out next to a glass dish of sticky pastel candies.

"No elevator," my mother apologizes, and she begins up the metal staircase, Min behind her, silent on the steps.

My father has afternoon classes and is not home, but my mother hollers out his name as she unlocks the door, anyhow, says, "He's gone," as she lets Min inside. She has not had the chance to clean, and the smell of last night's hamburger is still in the air. My father's bathrobe is slung over the couch, and his morning coffee cup and empty breakfast plate are still on the table across the room.

Min does not step far inside, but stands near the door, her coat and hat still on, her hands clasped in front of her. She moves her eyes over the room, over the couch and the little TV, the dining table with its two seats and its baby high chair, and then she looks at my mother. "It's nice," she says.

My mother takes Min's coat and hangs it on the rack, shows Min to the table, and moves to the kitchen to set water on the stove for tea. She stands at the sink as the water heats. "This will just take a minute," she calls to Min. The tea she finds in the cupboard is Lipton, and because she cannot stand the thought of offering Min a teabag, she fills the mugs at the stove, then throws the wet teabags into the trash. She doesn't have a tray, and so it takes her two trips to carry the tea to the table, first Min's mug and then her own. The tea is too strong and too hot, but both my mother and Min lift their mugs again and again to their mouths, taking small sips and not speaking.

The warm afternoon light coming in through the windows begins to fade, and the sky outside pales and then whitens, seems to harden like the thin crust of an eggshell, the way it does when the temperature drops.

"Well," Min says when she has emptied her mug, "I appreciate your invitation today." She smiles and stands. At the door, she turns and looks once more around the room—at the softening figures of the furniture, and the photographs of my parents' wedding hung on the wall above the television set. At my mother still seated near the window. "Your home is very cozy," she says. "I can see you and your family here." She pulls on her coat and hat and leaves.

From the window, my mother watches as Min waits on the street below for the bus. Min stands alone near the street lamp, her back to my mother. It is only a few moments before the bus arrives, and Min climbs the wide steps and disappears into the crowd of other people inside.

In the evening, my mother and father sit beside each other on the couch, the television on but silent, a textbook open on my father's lap.

"I had tea with a friend today," my mother says. She is eating a bowl of ice cream, and it is cold enough in her mouth to raise goose bumps on her arms.

"Oh," he says, and he looks pleased. He has many friends on campus. He has brought other graduate students home for meals or drinks, has invited large groups over for holidays. "A nurse?" he asks, and my mother nods. He reaches out and lays his palm against her belly for an instant, then against her thigh. "I bet she's nice," he says. "You should have someone nice to talk to there—at work. Someone you can relate to."

"Yes," my mother says. "That would be nice."

My father smiles again.

Beside him, my mother doesn't say any more, but finishes her dessert. She feels the warmth of his hand on her leg and considers his long fingers and their fine nails. She has seen new mothers at the hospital examining their babies' hands, counting fat digits, exclaiming over their children's squeezed faces and assigning family resemblance. Vanity, she used to think, finding *her eyes* or *his nose* on the child's undistinguished face. But it's simpler than vanity. It's a kind of self-protective instinct. Those mothers are determining their ownership. They're looking for signs of belonging in their infants' strange and water-wrinkled forms.

My father shifts as he continues his reading, presses his shoulder against hers when he lifts his hand to turn a page.

The day I am born, it snows again. My mother leaves the hospital after her shift and steps out into the flakes falling heavy and downy, softer than the earlier snows, padding the tree branches and the roof-tops and the pavement of the parking lot in several inches of white. She bundles her coat around herself and moves down the sidewalk, away from the university and toward Min's apartment. All day she has had a pain in her legs and in her back, a heaviness behind her knees as if they might give out. And her stomach has tightened like a hard fist beneath her cotton uniform top. She has seen women come into the hospital this way, at this early stage, and wait hours in the cold rooms of the maternity unit, and so, she has decided, she will simply wait elsewhere.

As she walks, she imagines the warmth of Min's bathtub, the float of the deep water, and the relief of being unburdened, even for only a few moments. A part of her wishes to slide into the water and stay, and she imagines the slits of gills opening along the sides of her belly, my form inside her drawing breath that escapes the gills in tiny, silvered bubbles.

Above her, the sky is low and pearled, and the branches of the oaks along the sidewalk seem to bend slightly earthward with the snow, ready to break.

When she reaches Min's apartment, my mother knocks and is let inside. She stands on the small rug at the door, her coat and hair damp. "I should have called," she says, "but the whole thing is really unbearable today."

Min looks at my mother's coat, which is wet at the shoulders and the hem and smells strongly of wool. "There is snow on your coat," she says. "Put it here." She points to the floor near the door, and my mother bends and lays the coat out along the carpet.

The lights in the room are all off except the small lamps by the couch, and the table is bare where the tea tray usually sits. Min looks at my mother, at her middle and the way her belly has dropped and hardened, and does not invite her to sit, to wait while she makes a cup of tea. "I'll fill the tub," she says instead, her face and her voice sharp. "You should go and have your bath." She disappears into the bathroom, and my mother hears the water running, hears Min opening the cupboard where she keeps the towels.

My mother crosses the room and stands near Min's large windows, looking out at the stretch of city below. The snow is falling faster now, and the sky is white and blank, the streets empty of people and silent.

When they first moved here, she and my father had not ever really known snow, had not known the way that snow can quiet a city and change it. The first snow that year fell at night, and they woke to it, a strange absence of sound in the bedroom around them and the odd, gray light of snow coming in through the window. They dressed in sweaters and boots and parkas, walked out into the snow, and waded through it down the empty street. Several inches had fallen, and the cool rising up from the earth chilled my mother's knees through her jeans and began to numb her calves. As they walked, they passed apartment buildings and houses with stoops banked in snow, the doors shut up tight against it and the windows of the buildings darkened by drawn shades. On campus the ironwork fence was latticed in white, and the buildings were unfamiliar, bulky shapes beneath their thick roofs.

"Like a new city," my father said, and my mother nodded.

They stood awhile looking up at the glitter of light on the snow-burdened tree branches, the blanked faces and snowy shoulders of the stone gargoyles guarding the campus buildings. Then my mother reached for my father's hand and took it, slipped their two hands together into the warmth of his pocket as they walked home.

Min reappears from the bathroom, and my mother steps away from the window. "The tub is filling," Min says.

"Did you want to sit first?" my mother asks. "We could sit while we wait."

Min looks at my mother as if she does not understand why my mother has come. "You should call your husband," she says. "You should have your bath." Min moves her eyes over the stark space of her front room—the white couch and the bare surface of the table.

"I'll call him after the bath," my mother says as she starts down the hallway, and Min nods.

In the bathroom, my mother closes the door and undresses, then sits down on the ledge of the tub to wait for the basin to fill. She looks at her belly, where the skin seems thinner and more translucent now that the constrictions of labor have begun and are tightening like a wide band around her middle. On the other side of the door, Min clears her throat. "You'll be quick?" she asks. She is not worrying about a birth in her bathtub, my mother knows; she is worrying about my father. He will arrive at her apartment in a few moments, and Min is considering the wet mess his feet will make of her carpet, the disruption of his presence in her household.

"You okay in there?" Min says from the other room. Behind the noise of the running faucet, her voice sounds distant. "You still okay?"

Beneath the skin of her belly, my mother feels the familiar shape of an elbow, a heel—maybe a hand—and touches her abdomen, imagines that she and I are palm to palm. "I'll be fine," my mother says.

She leans forward to turn off the tap.

Years later, when I am old enough to ask about this day, my mother will tell me that she didn't get into the bathtub. That she reached down and drained the water, pulled on her clothes and called my father, thanked Min, then took the elevator down to the lobby to wait. "It was an anxious wait," she'll say, telling me that she worried the weather would slow my father, remembering how he entered the lobby of Min's building covered in snow, a duffel bag of her hospital things in his arms. "He came right in to get me and we went to the hospital," she'll say.

In reality, however, it was she who went out to him. She buttoned her coat to the neck and pushed against the glass door of Min's lobby and walked out onto the street. For a moment, she wasn't sure she would know him, his shape changed by his big parka and the snow falling so heavily that it had become difficult to see at any distance. But when he rounded the corner at the end of the block, she called out to him. "I'm here," she called. She walked toward him, taking large strides until she reached his side, then leaned her weight against his offered arm.

DANGEROUS WOMEN

THAT WINTER I TOOK A POSITION as Professor Anton's assistant and began spending my afternoons in the narrow attic office at his house, sorting his mail and reading the dullest of my classmates' papers. There was snow outside—more snow every day, it seemed—and I could hear it pressing against the pitched roof of the professor's house, the strange, slight compression, like tissue paper crumpled in a hand or the stiff wrinkle of a taffeta skirt. When I stood from my work at the professor's desk to look out the window, I could see the spire of the college's chapel, the library's blocky roofline, the peaked upper story of my own dorm; but these things seemed far away, the campus another world entirely. Here, just below the window, the stand of pines that lined the professor's lawn fenced the house from the street and what lay beyond it. There was a birdbath in the yard, and the sparrows liked to line up along its cement lip looking at their own frosted reflections like other birds trapped, suspended in the frozen water.

In the beginning, the professor was gone most afternoons when I arrived, and the house was empty. He'd given me a key when I took the job, and so I developed a routine of letting myself inside and making a cup of tea on the stove in the dark kitchen, then taking my tea upstairs to the attic to begin the stack of work he'd left for me. The office smelled like wax and paper, and like the wool sofa he'd told me he kept there for naps. I liked to imagine that he lay there sleeping while I worked, an arm raised above his head and his face turned into the crook of his elbow, his pale hair messed when he woke. I was a junior that year and had taken several of his classes, had watched the way he moved back and forth across the front of the room while he lectured—long strides and wide gestures, as if the literature sent tremors through his body as he talked. And when he now and then lifted the textbook to read from it, I'd noticed the way he held the book in both hands, cradled it, then slid a finger in between its pages, opening to the section he'd marked. When I worked in his office, I imagined him taking my hands in his own. I imagined him touching my face. His fingers would smell like the deep crease of a book's spine, just the way the office smelled, the way my clothes smelled when I left his house to trudge back to the dorms. I thought these things, and then was guilty over thinking them, and I tried to remind myself that he was my teacher, my boss, a man as old as my father. That I was letting my mind run foolish.

One afternoon, on campus, the professor called out to me just as I started toward his house. "Wait," he yelled. "Dorothy!" I turned, and he jogged toward me. His figure was trim and tall in his sweater and wool jacket, and he had his leather bag slung over one shoulder, a black knitted cap on his head. He stopped when he neared me, his breath coming quickly, and took my wrist in his cold hand. "I thought I could catch you," he said. "You're on your way to my office, yes?

I'm headed home, too." He walked beside me across the field that stretched out in the center of campus. In the fall, there would have been boys playing soccer on the grass, girls on blankets with their books opened in front of them and their eyes on the game. But this was January, and we were the only two on the field, our feet making shallow tracks in the untouched and starch-white snow.

The campus was small—the buildings brick and old and academic—and was bordered by several quiet, narrow streets lined with the squat and well-kept houses of the faculty. It wasn't unusual to be invited to a professor's home for dinner, or to have a final class in an instructor's front room. The school encouraged such familiarities, in fact. But I was awkward walking home with Professor Anton. When we reached the edge of campus, I glanced behind us as we stepped off the curb, looking for anyone who might have noticed us together. We walked down the short streets toward his house without speaking, the only sound the crunch of our footsteps on the packed snow of the sidewalk.

As we arrived at his house, he stepped ahead of me in the drive and up the stoop. I could still feel the cool of his fingers against my wrist when he unlocked his front door, and I wished that he would touch me again—a hand to my shoulder or my back, a hand in my hair. But he simply held the door open and told me to come in and make myself comfortable.

He turned on lights as he moved through the house, flicking on the lamps in the front room, lighting the overheads in the kitchen. "You want something?" he asked. "You make tea, don't you? I see the bags in the trash."

"Should I have asked about that? I could have asked." I followed him into the kitchen then, but stood with my coat still on, my pack on my back.

"Dorothy," he said, smiling as if I were ridiculous. "You're so passive." He filled the kettle and went to a cupboard, found a box of Darjeeling and two mugs.

"I think it's all an act—your wallflower routine," he said, and my face warmed. "I see you sitting in the back of my classroom, silent as a mouse. But I know you've got all sorts of thoughts fluttering around in your head." He looked at me directly. "You look like a girl with thoughts. I'll begin to take it personally if you refuse to share them with me." He took the kettle from its burner and filled our mugs with water that hissed and steamed as it hit the ceramic.

The professor picked up his tea and moved out of the kitchen. "Take off your coat," he said. "I'll be waiting for you upstairs."

I stood a moment and listened for his feet on the staircase, then slipped off my coat and folded it into my backpack, carried the pack to the front room to set out of the way near the door. I hadn't looked at the front room in the light—it would have seemed too forward to come into the empty house and turn on lamps, too much a trespass. The room, I saw now, though, was cluttered, books stacked in piles along the walls and on the coffee table, the heavy furniture draped with blankets, and a batiked sheet spread like a tablecloth over the end table in the corner. There were paintings on the walls: a fruiting tree; a print in bright colors featuring a blue man in what looked to me like Indian dress, a woman at his side. And on the mantel, beneath a wide mirror, a photograph of a younger version of the professor standing with his arm around a pretty, dark-haired girl. The professor's eyes met the camera's focus, but the girl looked at him.

There were plants, as well—spider plants with long vines hanging in pots from the ceiling, a tray of African violets in glass dishes on the window ledge beside a potted narcissus, an amaryllis with a deep red bloom leaning heavily and about to snap its stalk. I wanted to walk the room and touch everything, but the professor called to me from the top of the staircase. "Are you lost?" he said, and I collected my tea and followed him up to the attic.

His class this term was mythology literature—fairy tales and ancient myths and fables. We'd read Aesop and the Greeks, and had lately moved on to the Grimm Brothers. I thought I remembered the stories from childhood, but the professor had assigned the original versions, and they were darker than I recalled, violent and odd. The girl who is turned out of her father's house because her beauty tempts him; the queen who poisons her stepdaughter with tainted combs; the seven sons turned into seven ravens by a father's fit of rage. These were the professor's favorites.

In his office, he sat in the desk chair and gave me the couch. He opened the Grimm book in his lap and picked up a pen to add to the notes he'd already scribbled along the tops of the pages and down the margins. Instead of getting to work, though, he turned to me. "What did you think of the last story?" he asked. "You wouldn't say in class, but I know you have an opinion. Come on and tell me now. Just the two of us—no risk."

"They're not what I thought," I said. "The stories. I remembered them differently, I mean. I remembered them as children's stories, but they're not." It was cold in the office, and I tucked my hands beneath my thighs, sat with my knees pressed together and my arms close to my sides.

He leaned forward and turned on the desk lamp, so that it cast a small circle of light on the desk and radiated a halo onto the sloped ceiling.

The professor nodded. "I suppose that's a compliment. I mean, you're not quite a child anymore, are you, Dorothy?"

"I didn't mean it like that. I wasn't expecting bedtime stories." I flushed again, and he smiled.

I had overheard one of the other girls in class say that his smile was sexy. *Like he's just done it,* she said. *Like he's still thinking about it.* It was a cat-got-the-bird smile, only when he turned it on me, I felt it was me he had swallowed, and I looked down into my hands.

"Well," he said, and sat back in his chair, "I think they're great soap operas, honestly. The drama of the betrayal. The family struggle. Jealousy running like fault lines beneath every household, and every mother wanting her daughter's heart boiled and served on a platter, just so she can taste the girl's youth," he said. He crossed his legs and raised his arms, knitting his fingers together behind his head. "Just to eat the girl's beauty," he said. He grinned. "Fairy tales are great for their human drama."

Professor Anton sat still another moment, then swiveled his chair around, away from me, to face the desk. "We're reading 'Ashputtel' next, and 'Snowdrop.' Nothing you expect them to be. Nothing like the Disney versions," he said. "We're going to defile Disney." He closed the Grimm book and set it on the desk, then fished a stack of multiple-choice exams from the pile of papers there. "You can score these downstairs if you want," he said. "I'm going to be working here today." He handed me the papers and a red pen without looking up at me, and I left the room.

The next time I arrived at the house to work, I found Mrs. Anton on the couch in the front room, the lights off and the curtains drawn as usual, but a fire in the fireplace, a stack of raw kindling lying in a pile on the tile hearth.

"I'm sorry," I said. I stood with the door still open, my hand on the knob.

"Close the door," she said. "You're letting in the cold." She had been lying down, sleeping. When she sat up, her makeup was smudged at the corners of her eyes, and her dark hair had come loose from its pins and fell sloppy around her face. She motioned for me to shut the door, then stood, but didn't step toward me, didn't offer to shake my hand or introduce herself.

"This is when I work. I work from three to five," I said. "But I can go if you'd rather."

"I knew he had a girl. Someone mentioned it. It's fine." She stood looking at the room around her as if disoriented, still asleep, and when she didn't say any more, I climbed the stairs to the attic and shut the door.

In a moment, I heard the sounds of her moving in the kitchen two floors below me—cupboards opened and shut, and the metallic clatter of pots and pans.

Until this afternoon, I had believed Professor Anton's wife was nothing but a figment of school gossip. She was never in town, and so had never actually been seen; and it was rumored that they weren't even really married anymore—that there'd been a falling-out, that he'd told her to go or she'd left him. I'd heard that she traveled the world and came back only occasionally, when he called her and begged, or when she could no longer stay away. She had been his student at one point, fifteen or twenty years ago, when he was just out of graduate school and new on campus, and he had nearly lost his job over her, because she would not leave him, or maybe because he could not give her up.

She was the girl from the photo in the front room—I recognized that. She still had the same wide-set eyes and dark hair, the same face, though it had narrowed over the years and looked pinched now, and drawn.

Upstairs in his office, I read the list of tasks the professor had left for me, but I couldn't concentrate, and so I stood and went to the attic window. It was snowing outside again, thin, feathery flakes like white ash that fluttered in circles of breeze before landing on the dark boughs of the pines and the naked branches of the sycamore further out in the yard. The snow dampered the light in the room. It colored the shadows that fell from the desk lamp and turned the trinkets on the bookcase a sooty gray.

She won't tolerate this weather, I thought. She looked to me like a fragile, birdy sort of woman, the kind too easily cold, too often irksome and whiny and self-involved. I could see her complaining about his long hours on campus. I could see her preening and plotting so he would pay her more attention, and I was certain now that it was he who asked her to go each time she left on one of her trips—because she had become unbearable finally. Because she didn't suit him at all anymore.

I turned my back to the window and sat down, but before I could start on the afternoon's work, I heard her on the stairs, and then the door opened. She looked down at me. "Do you know this kitchen?" she asked. "He's moved things. I can't find anything." She stood stooped beneath the low ceiling of the room—her hair long over her shoulders and her eye makeup tidied—and waited for me to get up and follow her. In the kitchen, the cupboard doors were opened, the tableware and wineglasses and the clutter of plastic and metal bowls visible. She had rummaged through the food in the cupboards, and boxes of dried noodles and cans of cling peaches and green beans, jars of asparagus and honeyed apricots sat out on the countertops.

"He moves things when I go," she said. "He can't keep order. He's not a householder, though I suppose you gathered that based on the state of his office." She stood with her arms crossed over her chest, surveying the mess. "I used to dismiss it as artistic preoccupation," she said. "He's just a slob, though. He believes books can be homes."

"He's an amazing teacher, though," I said, but she ignored me, turning a slow circle and peering into the cupboards again.

"I'm looking for a ginger grater," she said, "and a rice cooker. And I'm exasperated. You look now." She turned and left, and I stood in the bright kitchen alone.

I wasn't certain if she meant for me to go through their things, but when she didn't return, I got on my knees on the tile floor and searched the lower cabinets until I found the rice cooker tucked away in a corner, its lid dusty. I found the grater in a drawer cluttered with odds and ends—matchboxes and loose pennies, a garlic press and a spool of twine. I washed the rice cooker and dried it, set it beside the grater on the counter, and walked back upstairs to finish my work for the evening.

When I came down again in an hour's time, she was in the kitchen, her hair up now and an apron on over one of the professor's shirts. A pot on the back burner of the stove let off steam. "You found everything I couldn't," she said. "Already a smarter girl than I ever was."

"I'm glad I could help."

Mrs. Anton nodded. "Of course you're a help, Dorothy. Your name is Dorothy, isn't it? I called the English office and told them Tom's girl was here. He always has a girl. I don't remember the last one's name." She turned her attention to her dinner and didn't look up at me again as I buttoned my coat and let myself out of the house.

In my dorm room that night, the blinds open to the dark windows so that I could look out on the field and the snow still falling, I read the story the professor had assigned. Ashputtel, the cinder girl, is made to work in the ashes of her stepmother's fires. Until one day, when the house fills with birds—sparrows and ravens and finches—and the birds pick at the girl and tear off her ruined clothes, and dress her in something better suited to a woman meant to be a prince's bride.

* * *

For several afternoons I worked without seeing either the professor or his wife. I wondered if she had left again, but then I would find her things: a hairbrush tangled with her dark hair lying on the bathroom counter; her red coat draped over the back of the sofa. And one afternoon their bedroom door was open, so I could see their wide, unmade bed, and a nightgown lying in a satin heap on the floor near the night table. I could smell her in the house, too—her perfume, like hothouse flowers, and the scents of her cooking. The house smelled of onions now, and of garlic and meat. I closed the attic door when I went to work each afternoon, and propped open the window so that the breeze could drift in, and with it the stiff scent of cold air. I sat with my coat on and quickly finished my editing or grading, then left early.

One afternoon she was home again, though, and called to me when she heard the front door open and shut. "I'm here," she said, and I moved through the kitchen and down the hallway following her voice, passing a series of closed doors until I found her in a glass room at the very back of the house.

There were space heaters on in the room, and the glass was beaded with condensation, the bit of snow that had fallen on the glass ceiling softening in a pale blue-gray melt. Outside, the afternoon light was already low, the yard dark where the trees met at the edge of the property line. She had lit lamps at the ends of the wicker sofa where she sat with her feet up on a small table, a glass of wine there at her heels. She looked warm, her sweater unbuttoned at the neck and her feet in socks but no slippers.

"I would have knocked if I had known you were home," I said from the doorway.

"It's fine. I told you before, I'm used to Tom's girls coming in and out at all hours. I stopped worrying about being caught in my pajamas or seen without my makeup long ago." She shrugged.

"I didn't know you had a greenhouse back here," I said.

"Not a greenhouse, a sunporch." It had originally been just a porch, she told me, though she wanted to use it in the winter, and so the professor had glassed it in for her, even the roof. When it snowed, he had to get up on a ladder and sweep the snow off the glass with a broom to prevent any cracking. "He should do these things," she said. "It's good for him to have chores like that—chores other people do without consideration. He has to remember to do it even when I'm gone." She smiled.

There were plants in pots along the floor and on tiered metal shelves, plants hanging in pots from hooks screwed into the beams of the ceiling. "These are mine," she said. "A taro plant." She pointed to a large pot in the corner, a plant with big, heart-shaped, pleated leaves. "A Eucharist lily, a Eucrosia, lady's slippers." She nodded at each as she mentioned it, and then turned to a green metal cage in which sat two doves the color of gray flannel. "They don't have names," she said. "They're not like pets, birds. Tom bought them for me a couple of years ago as a gift, but I haven't named them. Sometimes I take them out and let them fly around, but today they should stay in the cage. I don't feel like dealing with them just now." The birds sat together on a suspended perch, their black eyes glassy and unmoving and intent on her.

"You could sit," she said, and gestured to a cushioned chair in the corner.

"I'm sure Professor Anton has left me work to do," I said. "I should go get started."

"I was his assistant, you know. He was young then. It was his first year teaching, and he didn't know what to do with me. He gave me busywork, tedious little things he could have done himself. Is that what he does now? Are you bored, Dorothy?"

I shifted, let my pack slide down my arm to rest on the floor. "It's fine," I said. "The professor and I get along pretty well."

Mrs. Anton leaned forward to pick up her wine. "Let me guess what he has for you. Lecture notes to type—he never learned how to do it. I still type his conference papers for him. I typed his book." She sipped from her wine. "Mail shuffling. Books to return to the library." She winked at me. "He's always very grateful, though, isn't he? Even for these small things." Mrs. Anton sat up and put her feet on the floor. "I remember," she said. "It hasn't been so long that I don't remember how it was at first."

I stayed still, listening to the sound of the doves edging along their perch, their claws grating on the wooden bar. They moved together, back and forth, never lifting a wing, in what seemed a pointless exercise.

"I should really go," I said.

"I'm thinking of having a party. I thought you could help. There'll be things to do—invitations and food to order, probably a cake."

"Is it his birthday?" I asked. I picked up my pack again and transferred its weight from one shoulder to the other. I had brought my homework this afternoon, and the hard edges of my books dug into my back.

"No," she said. She stood and walked ahead of me out of the room, bending to yank the cords on the heaters so that they shut off. "Just a party. It gives me something to do."

In the kitchen, she set her wine on the counter and opened the refrigerator, pulled out an onion, a cluster of wilting fringe-headed celery, a package of hamburger that dripped blood on the counter when she dug a fingernail beneath its plastic wrap to tear it open.

"Don't mention it to Tom," she said. "I like to surprise him." She looked up at me, nodded as if we'd agreed on it, then turned to face the sink and wash the celery.

"You should stay for dinner, Dorothy," she said, her back to me now. "I'll set you a place."

I worked in the attic until she called for me, then came down to the table that she had prepared with three plates, three red cloth napkins, three white taper candles flickering in pewter holders. She carried a lidded casserole dish to the table and placed it on trivets, poured wine into each of the three glasses and motioned for me to sit. "We'll wait for him," she said.

The dining room windows faced the yard—the birdbath and the pines—and outside the sky seemed lowered, the clouds gray-lipped with evening and thick and flat. A wind buffeted the boughs of the pines.

We sat—me with my hands folded in my lap, and Mrs. Anton across the table drinking her wine—until the professor arrived and filled the empty chair between us.

"Dorothy's joining us," Mrs. Anton said. She smiled at the professor over the flames of the candles. "I'm sure you don't mind."

"She invited me," I said, looking to the professor, but he seemed at ease, reaching for the bottle of wine across the table and pouring himself a glass.

Mrs. Anton stood then and lifted the lid on the casserole so that a vapor of steam rose and the smell of her dinner filled the small room: onion, black pepper, a spice I couldn't identify that burned in my mouth when I took my first bite. I reached for my wine and swallowed one gulp and another, my face warming with the alcohol.

While we ate, Mrs. Anton spoke only to the professor, asking him questions about his day, what he had taught, what paper he would send to a conference he wanted to attend. She ate very little, but served him a second helping, sat with her elbows on the table and her chin in her hands as he spoke, her eyes dark and glossy and fixed on him.

I excused myself before she could serve dessert, thanking her, glad to be able to go.

"I'll walk you out," the professor said.

"No, that's okay," I said. I looked to Mrs. Anton, who had sat back in her chair and watched us. "Really. I'll be fine." But the professor stood, letting his napkin fall to the floor. He touched his hand to the small of my back, so that I flushed and turned my face away from his wife as he escorted me out of the room.

At the door, he helped me into my coat, then put on his own, wrapped a scarf around his neck, and opened the door to the low light of the porch lamp and the stoop.

"I'm fine," I said. "She has dessert. You should stay."

The professor took my elbow, though, and led me down the steps. "It's dark," he said. "She can wait."

He looped my arm into the crook of his own, and walked close enough that I could feel the warmth of him through my jacket as we rounded the corner at the end of his block and continued toward campus.

"You two must have cooked all afternoon for me," he said. His breath was visible. It rose in small clouds that drifted up, dissipating, toward the bare tree limbs above us, the dark sky.

I didn't correct him, didn't tell him that I'd had nothing to do with it. I might have made him such a dinner, if she were not in the way. I might still, once she left again, as I was sure she would. Now I just leaned into his arm, moving in step with him at his side until we reached the edge of campus. "A lovely dinner," he said then, stopping, and I wanted him to take my hand, to kiss my palm or the tips of my fingers, but instead he said good-bye and told me to sleep well. I crossed the lawn to my dorm and stood watching him until he turned the corner at the end of the block.

I imagined that Mrs. Anton had given up on him, had risen from the table and taken the dishes to the kitchen, wrapped the dessert she'd made in plastic and put it in the freezer for another night. But then I thought better of it.

Mrs. Anton would still be waiting when he returned. She would seat him again, offer him another glass of wine, bend over him to scoop white lumps of ice cream into his bowl, and dish him a spoon of the cherries she had sugared and warmed on their stove. She would not mention me, but would sit in her own chair as he ate, her wine-glass refilled and the candles melting soft and disfigured at the center of the table.

After that evening, Mrs. Anton was nearly always home when I arrived. She rushed me through the professor's work and then called me to the dining table, where I sat addressing the stiff invitations she had bought, or to the kitchen, where she offered me samples of the hors d'oeuvres she was thinking of serving at the party—samosas wrapped in tidy pastry bundles, deviled eggs, apple tarts small enough to be eaten in one bite. She did not eat anything herself, but wanted to know exactly what I tasted. "There's lemon zest in that tart," she said. "Do you taste lemon? Should you taste more lemon?" I chewed, shook my head. Everything was just right.

Some afternoons, we got into her brown station wagon and drove to the market across town, or to the florist's. She dressed to go out, putting her long hair up into a complicated knot at the back of her head, fastening a necklace around her throat, and tying the belt on her car coat taut at her waist. These errands weren't always for the party, and I wasn't certain I ought to have gone along, but when once I said I thought I would stay, that the professor had left more than the normal amount of grading for me to do, she nodded. "That's fine," she said. She slid her arms into her coat and cinched the tie, clasped her purse shut. "I wonder how it looks that he's asked you to be in our home," she said. "Unattended." She looked at me.

"I guess I could come," I said then, and I followed her out to the car.

Within a month's time, the weather had warmed just enough for the snow to melt, and instead of driving across town to buy groceries one Friday afternoon, she took a different route, winding up and down the residential streets beyond campus until a park came into view—a broad, oak-lined drive, and in the distance, an ornate, white fountain drained of its water for the winter. Mounded flower beds were scattered here and there, each tucked beneath a blanket of burlap. She pulled into the parking lot and stopped, got out and waited for me to do the same. "I used to run here," she said. "When I was your age. When I was a student, I liked to come here to escape." She had on heels, but started down the slope of a gravel path, her purse held tightly to her body beneath the bend of her elbow.

The park was empty except for a mother and little girl several yards from us across the grass, and a young couple against the white bark of a sycamore, their faces pressed together and the boy's hands disappeared into the girl's back pockets.

"There's an aviary," Mrs. Anton said. She walked quickly and kept a few paces ahead of me. She pointed. "There." Beyond the boxy fence of a hedge, I could see the aviary's netted roof, large and round and peaked in the middle by a pole like a tent. There were birds flapping beneath the netting, small birds, I thought. And then something large-bodied—a goose maybe—arced up and dove again, a streak of dark feathers.

As we got closer, I could see that the aviary was actually a building—a cement-block center like the hub of a wheel, and walls that extended like spokes to make cells that separated the birds' nesting areas. The outer wall was nothing but chicken wire, and when we reached it, Mrs. Anton crouched down and put her fingers through the holes, clucking her tongue at a pheasant hen, so that it scratched long cuts in the earth and squalled at us. The prettier male ignored the yelling, though, and came over, pecked the ground, and then, eyeing us, touched its beak to Mrs. Anton's fingers.

"I don't know how many species they have," Mrs. Anton said. "Nothing exotic. Wood ducks and mallards and swans, and a type of spotted chicken. Ring-necked pheasants like this one. And peacocks." She stood and dusted her hand on the thigh of her pant leg. "Did he tell you that story about the peacock?" she asked. "His dream. He dreamt he made love to a peacock. He grew feathers then. He became beautiful." She shrugged, and turned away from the birds, and began up the trail to the parking lot again. "He believes it's a mythical dream. That it makes him special. He likes the reaction it gets, and so he tells it to his class every year."

He had told us. He had described the bird and the sense of trans-figuration he felt even after he woke up—as if he'd been actually altered. *The feathers were long and luminescent,* he said. *A perfect blue. Try and imagine it. The body as a conduit for beauty.*

I had closed my eyes and tried to see what I thought he was seeing—an embrace, wings against my back—and then my own body changed, feathered and blue and stunning.

"Do you see it?" he asked again, interrupting. I opened my eyes and saw him leaning forward over his podium, grinning. "Can you imagine how beautiful I felt? I felt gorgeous."

Mrs. Anton and I walked back to the car and got in, then sat until the heater revved up and blew warm air against our ankles.

Beyond the windows, the park lawn was empty, the sky gone a smoky shade of gray.

"Where do you go when you leave?" I asked. I didn't turn my face to her.

Mrs. Anton was still, her hands on the unmoving wheel. "When I was your age I would have looked at my life now and thought it wonderful," she said. "I would have thought that when I met him."

Our breath had fogged the car windows. She looked at me. "You don't really want to know where I go when I leave," she said. "I know you, Dorothy. You want to know why I come back."

She pulled the car from its spot and drove toward campus again. When we arrived at the house she got out and crossed the lawn toward the door. "You've done enough work today," she said, her back to me. "You go on home now."

Over the weekend, I wrote a paper on the Grimms' version of "Snow White." In their story, though the queen tries again and again to ensure her stepdaughter's death, the girl lives, and charms her prince, and marries him. And the queen chokes on the bile of her own rage.

The assignment requested an analysis of the story's major character, but I wrote my paper on the queen. The queen as aging and ungrateful. The queen as jealous of her stepdaughter's youth and possibility. Envious of the girl's fine fortune in attracting a good man.

I didn't go back to the house the next week. I told the professor I was sick, skipped my classes, and lay on my bed in the dorm reading the work he had assigned, walking at dusk to the dining hall to collect an apple, a sandwich, a carton of milk that I carried back to my room to eat there.

One morning that week, while everyone else was in class, I tried to remember the roads Mrs. Anton had taken to get to the aviary. I left campus and walked, noting a blue house that seemed familiar, a child's tire swing in a front yard, a cluster of early white irises blooming in the garden on a corner lot. Eventually, the park's fountain came into view, and I crossed the street and moved to the edge of its empty pool. There were the three scalloped basins—each smaller than the one below it—and at the center of the fountain, the statue—three ladies, I could see now, poised on the top tier. The women wore loose gowns that left their white calves bare, bodices that revealed their pretty stone shoulders. Had there been water, it would have been bubbling at their feet, cascading tier by tier down to the wide, tiled wading pool. They were the muses, or Odysseus' sirens. Dangerous women.

I sat on the edge of the fountain and buried my hands in my coat pockets. The day was nearly warm, bright. The sky was a thin and washed-out blue. I thought I might see her if I sat long enough, that she might have decided to walk that morning as well. I wasn't certain what I would do if I saw Mrs. Anton, or what I would say if she called to me and I had to speak. Maybe I would repeat her own words to her. *You've done enough. You should go now.*

From the aviary, there was the sound of birdcalls, but no one appeared over the rise of the hill, and so I got up and walked back to campus.

Over the next couple of weeks, I gave the professor excuses for not returning to the house. The cold I had was lingering; I was suddenly swamped with essays to write; I had signed up for the drama club and had a play to rehearse. These were lies, all of them, but he didn't question me, and I was relieved not to have to face his wife.

The day of the party, however, Mrs. Anton called the dorm. "I looked up your number. The department had it," she said. "I'm going to need your help this afternoon, Dorothy. I have flowers and food and twenty bottles of wine here, and I'm going to need you to come over to help me set up."

I paused, and there was the sound of her sigh on the line.

"Please," she said. "I'd like you to come." She hung up then, and I stood with the phone against my ear a moment, wishing I had been able to tell her no.

At three I folded my only black dress on top of a pair of black heels in my pack and walked to the Antons' house. She was there waiting when I knocked, her face pale without makeup and her hair long and uncombed down her back. She wore one of his shirts, the chest splattered with the spills of her cooking, and when she let me in, she led me right to the kitchen. "I need you to set up trays," she said, and motioned to a stack of silver platters and then to the counter, where several cookie sheets of samosas and tiny quiches, washed vegetables and skewered strawberries sat. "They should look neat," she said.

As I worked, she moved behind me at the stove, simmering a plum sauce, opening and closing the oven door to check on the rise of the puff pastries. She had made cheesecakes that sat already cooling on racks near the sink; a mousse that she spooned into a crystal dish and put into the refrigerator; a cake that she iced with white frosting as I carried the last of the trays to the dining table and arranged them as she had directed beside the linen napkins, the stack of plates and rows of wineglasses.

"We should get dressed," she said then, and she took me upstairs and into her bedroom.

There was a blue dress on a hanger at the back of the bedroom door—a fine, iridescent blue, with a fitted waist and a taffeta skirt that would fall just above her knees. She disappeared with the dress into the bathroom, and a moment later opened the door and stepped toward me, turning her back to ask for help with the zip. The dress flared at the skirt, and Mrs. Anton turned this way and that in front of the long mirror in the corner, watching the fabric feather out and then settle. When she seemed pleased with herself finally, she sat on the bed and slid a shoe box from beneath the bed skirt, putting on the pair of blue heels it held. "You're not dressed," she said. "I hope you brought something. I won't be able to lend you anything—we're not the same size." She moved into the bathroom again and closed the door, and I could hear the tap running and then the small plastic clasps of her makeup cases snapping shut as she put on her face.

The bedroom looked like him to me—his blazers on a coat tree in one corner, his books on the table near the bed, along with a pair of reading glasses, a tumbler still half-full with last night's water. The impression of his head was still on the pillow on his side, and when I sat on the edge of the bed to untie my shoes, I considered that he had been beneath the blankets only a few hours before, that he would be beneath them again later.

I turned my back to the bathroom and eased off my shirt, pulled my dress from my pack and slid it on over my shoulders and waist before unfastening my jeans and stepping out of them. I had forgotten nylons, and my feet felt odd when I fit them into my shoes, too naked. There was the sticky sound of skin against the synthetic soles inside when I walked.

I was at the mirror when Mrs. Anton opened the bathroom door and came out, the scent of her perfume drifting into the room with her, her hair pinned up and a string of black pearls around her neck, black pearl studs fastened to her earlobes. She stood behind me, her image in the mirror. "That's a sensible dress," she said.

I nodded and met her eyes in the mirror. I combed my fingers through my hair and wished I had remembered to bring a lipstick, a cake of blush.

"That's fine," she said. "You'll be filling wineglasses. No one will notice your hair."

The professor didn't come home until the house had filled with guests. Mrs. Anton had invited his colleagues, other professors from the English department, and professors I had never met—someone from theater, someone from religion, a man who told me he was the visiting ceramist as I filled his glass in the low-lit dining room. Mrs. Anton wanted me to stand near the food table. She'd given me a hand towel and had watched me practice pouring the wine, showing me how to tip, then twist the bottle to keep from dribbling, demonstrating how full each glass should be before leaving me to the task. I could hear her voice now as she moved from room to room, visiting with the guests. I was the only student at the party.

When Professor Anton did arrive, she took his arm and led him to the kitchen, where I saw her hand him a plate she had filled earlier and saved for him, a glass of white wine she'd kept cool in the fridge. He leaned toward her briefly and kissed her cheek, took the plate and the glass and walked away. At the kitchen counter, Mrs. Anton stood still a moment and watched him leave.

For a long time, I stood with a wine bottle in my hands, my eyes on the professor as he moved from conversation to conversation in the other room. It was a quiet party. People sat on the couches and stood in small groups talking about their classes, their work. There wasn't any music playing in the background, just low voices, the polite sound of forks against plates.

Finally, the professor crossed the room toward me. "Well, this is dull, isn't it, Dorothy?" He held out his wineglass, and I picked up a fresh bottle, uncorked it, and poured for him. "I don't know why she thought I would enjoy this." He looked out to the front room where Mrs. Anton stood with the ceramist and another woman, then he nodded in the direction of the kitchen. "Come with me."

I followed him past the wreckage of empty plates and bottles in the kitchen and down the hall to the sunporch. "I've seen this room," I said. "Your wife showed me her plants."

The professor ignored me, easing the door nearly closed, and sitting on the wicker sofa. He patted the cushion next to him for me to sit as well.

It was dark in the room. The light from the kitchen windows spilled out into the yard beyond the glass, but where we sat there was no light, and I could see the room only in shadow: the coiled and corded bodies of Mrs. Anton's plants, the long-stalked figure of an amaryllis, the dark hulk that was the birds' cage beneath a cloth drape. Above us, through the glass roof, a wrack of blue clouds was visible, a few stars as distant as the murmur of voices from Mrs. Anton's party. I wanted to forget the party. I wanted to forget that we were still in the same house. In this room, beside him, it was easy for me to believe that we were somewhere else entirely.

"It makes me think of Eden," I said. "This room. You forget there are walls." I sat in the corner of the sofa, my hip pressed against the armrest, but I could feel the weight of him near me, could smell on his breath the sweet ferment of alcohol. I was conscious of the fact that my legs were bare, and that I was sweating behind my knees.

From the cage, there was the rustle of wings—a soft, crinoline sound—and the professor stood and walked to the birds, lifted the sheet. "Doves," he said. He opened the cage door and stretched his hand inside, letting the birds jump from their perch to his wrist before withdrawing his arm. "Come here, Dorothy," he said. When I got to my feet and walked toward him, he leaned so that one of the doves fluttered and hopped onto my wrist, clung to me with its claws. The bird moved its feet up my arm, sidestepping, opening its wings in a way that made me catch my breath.

"Let him sit on your shoulder," the professor said. "He'll take your ear into his beak." On his own shoulder, the second dove bent her gray head to his, and I saw her touch her black beak to his ear, saw the flash of her dark tongue at the lobe.

"You're too tense, Dorothy. Relax." He stepped close and took my hand in his, ran his other palm along the inside of my forearm, back and forth over my skin. "Relax," he said. "The birds can sense anxiety. Let yourself relax."

His palm was cool, and my arm tingled and numbed where he touched it. I knew I ought to step away from him, return to the party and the wine, but I couldn't move. I imagined the white statues on the park's fountain, their frozen pose, and the Grimms' sleeping princesses—all of them stilled by romance.

On my shoulder, the bird loosened his grip and brushed his head against my neck, opened and closed his wings again, though slowly this time, so that I didn't flinch but felt the points of his feathers against my cheek, his beak picking at the neckline of my dress.

I closed my eyes.

"Tom," Mrs. Anton said. She had opened the door to the room and appeared in the doorway, her figure statuesque and dark against the bright light of the hall, the stiff triangle of her skirt sharper in silhouette. "Tom," she said again. "Professor Jenkins is asking after you. He read your paper in the journal." She kept her voice steady, the tone even, so that though I could not see her face, I could imagine her looking at him with a stony expression.

The professor backed away from me, squeezing my wrist an instant before letting go. "I'll only be gone a minute, Dorothy," he said low and beneath his breath.

"No, Dorothy," Mrs. Anton said. "You shouldn't wait." Her voice had hardened.

"We're talking, Laura," the professor said. "We're just talking. I'm telling Dorothy how much I love these parties you throw." He stood between us—Mrs. Anton and me—and grinned at me, then reached up to run a finger along the head and back of the dove still resting on his shoulder. The dove chortled a note like a deep whisper into his neck.

"Tom," Mrs. Anton said again. "There are thirty of your colleagues in the living room. It is completely inappropriate for you to be out here. With her." She paused. "You can't do this."

On the professor's shoulder, the dove warbled once and then twice more. She lowered her soft head and waited, her wings still, for the professor to stroke her as he had before. But when he reached up, the bird pulled back and struck at him with her beak, so that he jerked, and then swiped at her, and she flapped suddenly, in uneven panic, toward the ceiling, a streak of movement in the dark room. There was a dull thud against the glass, and the dove's body dropped to the floor.

The professor stopped. "She bit me," he said. "She bit me, Laura." He didn't move. He looked to his wife.

The bird lay on the floor.

When Mrs. Anton spoke now, her voice was soft. "It's going to be fine," she said. She stepped out of the doorway and into the room, turned on a lamp. "Don't move, Dorothy," she said. She reached toward my shoulder and took the other dove in both hands, pinning its wings to its sides until she had closed it back into the cage. Then she went to the second bird and knelt. The bird had broken its neck. It was a gray lump of feathers, its wings slack and opened awkwardly, its black eyes fixed on nothing.

"Is it dead?" the professor asked. "Laura, has it died?"

"I'll take care of things," Mrs. Anton said. "You should go. You don't have to see this." She nodded and smiled at him. "Tom," she said. "It's going to be okay." And when he left, she cupped her palms around the bird and scooped it up.

"I'm sorry," I said. I still hadn't moved. "Mrs. Anton, I'm so sorry."

She ran a finger over the bird's feathers, tucked its feet beneath its body.

"You know," she said, "I always think these parties will go well. I forget that Tom doesn't realize. The work. The obligation. I don't think he'll ever understand the effort." She closed a hand over the bird.

Her hair had slipped from its pins and hung in her face. Bent there near the floor, she seemed rumpled, the hem of her skirt dusty and the fabric less lovely in the bright lamplight, just an ordinary blue. She looked up at me.

"You wanted to know where I go when I leave," she said. "I go home. I visit my mother. She worries about me. I don't think she can imagine my life. She had something else in mind for me maybe." Mrs. Anton lifted her shoulders in a small shrug. "She's old now. I'll visit her again soon."

I nodded. It was cold in the room, though I hadn't noticed before. In the light I could see that the glass had fogged around the edges of each pane, and that the amaryllis bloom had drawn its petals closed for the night.

"I should rejoin the party," Mrs. Anton said. She took in a breath, and rose, then turned to lay the bird on the table, covering its body with an open magazine. "Everyone's had enough wine now, I'm sure, Dorothy," she said. "You can eat if you like, or you're free to go."

She moved ahead of me out of the room, but stopped at the door, shifting to face me again. "I've appreciated your help with tonight," she said. "I do appreciate it all."

Mrs. Anton left then, to find her husband, and in a moment I made my way through the guests to the front door, where I pulled on my coat and gathered my pack. Across the room, she stood beside him now, her arm around his waist, and his body leaning into her as they listened to Professor Jenkins going on about his own new book. Neither of them noticed when I opened the front door.

Outside, the air was cold against my bare legs. The drive was full of cars, so I crossed the lawn, my feet crushing footprints in the grass, which was rigid already with the falling temperature. In the center of the yard, the water in the birdbath was crusted in just a thin layer of ice, tendrils of frost feathering a delicate pattern across the surface, and the water beneath them liquid, but brown and clotted with leaves that had lain still all winter.

I walked out of the pine shadows toward the street. Above me, the sky was high and clear and smoky blue. In my pack, I found my socks and my jeans, and pulled them on under my dress. I traded the patent-leather heels I'd been wearing for my sneakers, and made my way back to the dorm.

BABY LOVE

THE BOYS WOULD STAY with their aunt while their parents went away for the week—a couple's vacation, their parents had revealed at the last minute, and they'd winked at each other over the boys' heads. The trip was a surprise to his brothers, but Emil, the youngest, had known about it. Earlier in the week, their mother had taken him with her to the mall to buy a new sundress and a swimming suit for the trip. The suit was a red bikini, the straps thin and crisscrossed over the narrow and freckled width of her back, and the bottom tied in knots at her hips. Emil sat with her purse on the bench in the dressing room, jangling his mother's keys and writing notes to himself on the carbon paper in her checkbook while she turned back and forth in front of the long mirror, appraising her reflection. At one point the salesgirl knocked and then opened the door. "Oh, Mrs. Porter," she said. "Isn't your husband loved." His mother grinned and nodded, told the girl she'd take the suit.

She smiled at Emil and pulled a Snickers bar out of her bag, breaking the candy inside its wrapper, then peeling back the end so that the slightly bigger half slid into Emil's palm. "We won't tell your brothers," she said, whispering. She twisted the wrapper, dropping the remaining candy into her purse. "No need to get everyone in a fuss now. We'll keep the trip a secret between us, won't we, Emil? A secret just between you, and Daddy, and me." She squatted down then and leaned forward, hugged Emil to her, and held him for just a moment. When he leaned into her hugs, Emil always smelled cinnamon on his mother's skin and in her dark hair, the smell of warm things, things delicious to eat. Then she stood again and changed back into her clothes.

In the car on the way to his aunt's, the city and the gray horseshoe of Puget Sound too distant to see even as a horizon line, Emil thought of the swimming suit inside his parents' suitcase, on top of the blue shorts his mother liked to wear to garden, and her yellow flip-flops, and the neat stack of his father's boxer shorts and balled white socks.

He sat in the backseat of the car, in the middle, squished between John's oversized kneecaps and long legs, and Danny's slump. John would go to high school in the fall, and Danny to the sixth grade, but neither was allowed to sit in the front when all of them rode together, because, their mother said, things had to be fair. Instead, she set her purse in the front seat. It was a big leather bag, in which Emil knew she had three red pens, a photo of each boy as a baby, and the other half of the Snickers bar that she had kept for herself.

Emil sat straight, craned his neck so that he might smell the scent of his mother. He would try to hold it in his nose if he could, save it while she was away. Danny elbowed him, though, and scowled. "You're over the line," he said, and pointed to the upholstery, drawing an invisible border between their seats with his finger so that Emil sat back in his place, folded his arms across his body, and touched his knees together, making himself small. He wished he could go on the vacation with his parents, leave his brothers to his aunt.

Aunt Virgi was his mother's older sister, a tiny woman with the features of a horse—droopy, sad eyes and a long, narrow face. Each time she'd visit—at Thanksgiving and on his mother's birthday— she'd hug each of the boys and then kiss their cheeks, so that they had to wait until she'd turned her back to scrub with the cuffs of their shirtsleeves at the lipstick marks she left. For Christmas, she sent them each a book and a package of white brief-style underwear that they thanked her for in the letters their mother made them write.

"Mom," Emil said. He reached forward and touched her elbow with his fingertips. "I don't want you to go."

His mother sighed. "Please don't start," she said. She moved away from his grasp, taking one hand from the steering wheel to flip down the visor mirror and run a finger along her lower eyelid where her mascara had smudged. "Don't start with me now, boys. Your father and I need this vacation."

"At least I got the house," Aunt Virgi said to Emil's mother after they'd arrived and the children had been sent to play. It was sunny outside, and through the sliding glass doors, Emil could see his brothers and cousins playing a game of T-ball on the lawn, but he didn't join them. He'd hung back, claiming a stomachache after the luggage and sleeping bags had been carried in from the car, and sat beside his mother at the kitchen table, a cool washrag over his fore- head and a glass of seltzer water in front of him. Aunt Virgi had set out a pitcher of red Kool-Aid and a plate of Oreos, but Emil could see there'd be no point in asking for cookies now. He sat quietly instead, the rag dripping chill water droplets down his temples as the two women drank their coffee and the other kids yelled and called to one another outside.

"Really," Aunt Virgi said again. "I'm glad he gave me that much." She was divorced, and still living with her three daughters in the house she and her ex-husband had moved into when they married. "I can just see me dragging the girls to a one-bedroom in some complex in Renton, which is about what I could afford on my own," she went on. "I can just see me like some horrible welfare case, coming home from work each night to feed them macaroni and cheese while we listen to the neighbors' domestic violence." She squinted her eyes when she laughed, stumped her fist against the table.

"It's a great house," Emil's mother said. She looked at Emil and lowered her voice. "You deserve it. You deserve everything after what he put you through."

Outside, Emil's brothers had the bat and the ball now, Danny crouching and winding his arm with each pitch, aiming low and hitting John's thigh and then his hip and then his crotch, until John took after him with the plastic bat, chasing him across the lawn and into the bramble that marked the edge of the property. The girls stood with their arms at their sides and watched.

Later, after the women had finished their coffee, Emil's mother called the others in, and they ate cookies, and then it was time for Emil's mother to go. Rob would be waiting for her at the airport, she explained, and she hugged Virgi and the girls, and then touched each of her boys on his head, ruffling his hair. They all went out to the driveway to wave good-bye, and she honked the horn as she pulled out, then honked again from the end of the street before turning the corner and disappearing.

The week without his mother began slowly. Emil tried not to count the days until her return, but he couldn't help it. By the end of the first day, he was bored and homesick, and Aunt Virgi's house was hard to get used to. There were reminders everywhere that it was a girls' house. There was pink carpeting and wallpaper in the bedrooms upstairs; and in the bathroom, drawers full of spongy hair rollers and sticky tubes of lip gloss that smelled like fruit and bubble gum but tasted waxy when Emil touched his tongue to their tips. Beneath the narrow bed he slept in, he found a box of Barbies, most of them naked, their hair wild and tangled, and their plastic arms and legs stiffly posed. And everywhere there was the smell of girls—not the spicy, comforting smell of his mother, but a sickly sweet smell instead, like cotton candy and toothpaste.

Emil had never really paid attention to his cousins before this visit, but now, having so many long hours to watch them, he decided he didn't like them at all. Aunt Virgi's girls each looked like a variation on Aunt Virgi. Each girl had red hair and a long face, though the oldest had wider eyes and a bigger nose than her mother. The middle girl had a large mouth that she opened whenever she laughed to reveal the shiny tracks of her braces. And the youngest girl, Abby, was the prettiest, but she was plump. Abby had turned eight just a month before Emil in the winter, but was taller than him by several inches, and could have pinned him in a wrestling match, no contest. Abby was the only one of his cousins Emil didn't mind. He felt badly for her, actually, for her freckles and fat legs, for the way her sisters taunted "chubby baby, chubby baby" across the dinner table at her that first night when Abby took a second helping of hamburger casserole. He felt a solidarity with her, and imagined himself standing up for her the next time her sisters teased. He could see himself stomping over to the older girls, pointing his finger hard and accusatory at them, but he couldn't quite come up with anything smart enough to say—something sharp and biting that would stun them into silence, keep Mary Louise from smirking and shut up Rebecca's shiny, metal laugh.

In the backyard, just off the patio, there was an aboveground pool that the girls' father had bought for them at the start of the summer, and the second afternoon of the boys' visit, they all put on their suits and climbed over the flimsy edges into the water. The water was cold, the pool small and too shallow for diving. And when they began to splash too much, Aunt Virgi yelled, calling from her lawn chair for them to quiet down before they gave her a migraine. The pool was all elbows and knees with six of them in it anyway, and so Emil ended up standing in one spot, dunking his head every few moments to practice holding his breath or opening his eyes beneath the water.

"Get out, Emil," Danny directed. "We're playing Marco Polo, and you're in the way." He made shooing motions with his hand, looked to John for reinforcement.

"Both of you get out," Mary Louise said. She made her way across the pool and lifted Abby, kicking, above the water. "Get out," she said.

"Mom!" Abby screamed until her sister set her down again. "Mom!"

But Aunt Virgi had a magazine open in her lap, a rum and Coke balanced on the arm of her lawn chair, and she simply raised her eyes for a moment and shrugged.

Abby looked to Emil and rolled her eyes just as he had seen her older sisters do. She moved to the pool's edge and waited for Emil to climb out before her, then hoisted herself up over the ladder behind him and stood on the top rung shivering and wringing out her pony-tail, snapping the legs of her suit down over her backside before step-ping to the grass and tucking her towel like a skirt around her waist.

The two of them then sat on the patio, the water that dripped from their hair spreading out in dark polka dots on the concrete. They wrapped themselves in their towels and watched the others' heads bobbing up and down above the rim of the pool's walls.

Emil thought of his mother and father. They'd gone to Florida. He'd never been to Florida but had seen it on a map at school—Florida all the way across the country, like a thumb stretching out into the

Atlantic Ocean. On the map, there were pictures of palm trees and oranges speckling the state, and now he envisioned his parents on a beach, sitting in the shade of two palm trees, a plate of orange wedges between them on the sand. His mother was in the red bikini, and his father was in his green swim trunks.

In Emil's mind, his father's face was not altogether formed, just a pair of eyes and a blur beneath a wide forehead and a head of curly gray hair. His father worked in the city at a bank, got on the bus every morning before Emil was even awake, and came home in the evenings just in time for dinner. He liked to watch *Jeopardy!* after that, calling out the answers with the contestants, and would get up from the TV at eight to read one book to Emil before bed, replacing the book in the bookshelf and turning out the light, shutting the door behind him as he left, so that the room went entirely dark. On the weekends, he played basketball with the boys in the driveway, and now and then Emil had seen him walk up behind their mother in the kitchen or the laundry room, put his hands on her hips or her backside in a way that made her turn suddenly and lean against him.

Picturing his parents on the beach in Florida, Emil saw his father lay his hand on his mother's bare stomach, saw his mother roll closer to him on the sand.

Emil stood up, his towel still around his shoulders, and looked to Abby. "Let's do something," he said, and she nodded in agreement, stood as well, and started across the lawn, motioning for him to follow.

At the edge of the lawn, the grass became taller, uncut and rangy. It brushed against Emil's knees as he made his way behind Abby toward the bramble. There were blackberry bushes and ferns then, alder and birch saplings that bent in sorry angles toward the ground.

"Watch the nettles," Abby said.

Neither of them had thought to put on shoes, and they walked on tiptoe, choosing the best and clearest spot to land each footstep.

Emil saw the glistening trails of slugs sliding off into the brush, and above his head, in the canopy of trees, the shapes of tent-caterpillar nests, ugly and gray. There was the distant sound of a creek, and the green smell of leaves—a smell that made Emil think of the Mason jars in which he and his brothers sometimes trapped worms or lady-bugs. The ladybugs fluttered at first, batting against the glass walls of the jar, then finally settled and in a few days stopped moving, their wings faded to orange and their bodies hardened into husks. The worms lay still until they dried and shrank. Once they'd caught a spider that spun a web between the lid and the floor of the jar and within days laid an egg sack that hung suspended there in the web, a fascinating mummy that Emil had to keep himself from poking open and destroying.

At the tree line, the ground dropped down into a ravine, and Abby stopped, bent forward, and wound her towel around her head like a turban. She began descending, holding on to low tree branches to steady herself. The ground here was muddy and wet, and it squished between Emil's bare toes as he followed her, grabbing the branches she had grabbed, fighting to keep from tripping on his towel.

"Put it on your head," Abby said. She'd turned a few feet ahead of him to wait and bent now, unraveling her towel and demonstrating how to rewind it. She held her hands up when she finished. *"Voilá,"* she said, like a TV magician.

"I'm fine," Emil said. He held his towel at his neck like a cape, grasping at an alder branch and losing his footing for a moment. When Abby turned her back again, he stopped and bent forward as she had done, wound the towel around his head so he'd have both his hands free.

The fort was tucked into a group of trees at the center of the ravine. The structure was rounded, like a beaver's dam or an igloo, the walls a tangle of blackberry bramble and some sort of creeping plant that had grown tall. When Abby reached it, she stood with her hands on her hips and grinned. "Go in," she said, and she waited for him to duck beneath the low entrance of drooping branches. Inside, the light was green—strained through a latticework of leaves and branches—and a space had been cleared on the ground, two flat rocks dragged in to serve as seats. Emil could stand straight at the center of the fort, and there was room inside for eight or ten people, at least.

"It's good, isn't it?" Abby said. "No one else knows about it." She seemed pleased with herself, and kept smiling as Emil took in the space.

"What do you do here?" he asked.

"I just sit," she said. "Sometimes I bring a book. You can't hear anyone once you're inside, and no one outside can see you."

"What do we do right now, though?"

Abby took her towel from her head and shook it, then spread it long over the dirt at the center of the fort and lay down, her hands behind her head. "Let's just lay out," she said. She closed her eyes. Her red hair had worked itself back into curls as it had dried, and it was splayed about her head in a tangled mess. Across the body of her suit, there were two shooting stars, their tails fat and edged in green glitter.

Emil spread his towel close to hers and lay down. He squinted so that the white light coming in through the spaces between the leaves above his head flashed and narrowed and widened, making a doily of lace on the ceiling of the fort. He concentrated until the sound of the jays and the robins calling—the tripping, water-run sound of the creek—became one strand of sound, and then hollowed out, silenced inside his head. Beside him, he could still hear Abby's breathing, though, a quiet in and out, and could smell the scent of bleach on both their bodies from the pool water, the scent of fabric softener on the towels beneath them. He could feel the heat of her body so near him, and when she moved, adjusting her towel beneath her, her hair brushed against his shoulder, raising goose bumps on his skin.

"It's good, right?" Abby asked again, lying flat on her back once more.

Emil nodded, his eyes still focused in a squint. "It's good," he agreed.

At school, Emil had developed a crush on a girl with brown braids and a red backpack. She rode his bus and got on one stop after him, always sitting in the seat just before Emil's, so that her braids draped over the metal seat back, their paintbrush ends swinging just above his knees with the movement of the bus. She was a year older than him and in the third grade. She wore her backpack slung over one shoulder, with a smaller, zippered bag that Emil guessed was a change purse or a pencil bag ribboned to one of the straps. In the mornings, he watched the front of the bus as it pulled to her stop, felt his breath catch in the back of his throat until she appeared at the bus steps. His face reddened, and he looked away as she walked toward him and sat down. Every morning he had to will himself not to touch the braids.

He had seen his brother John kiss a girl once, last summer, at the public swimming pool. The girl was tall and thin and she let John buy her a plastic cup of Coke and sit next to her on the pool deck while she drank it. When John spoke to her, the girl threw her head back to laugh, her mouth open so that her big, white teeth and her pink tongue were visible. She stood up when the lifeguards whistled closing time, and moved close to John, and then John touched her waist, and put his face to hers, and kissed her.

Emil had seen all of this from the shallow end of the pool, and he had played it in his mind over and over since, his vision narrowing in on the girl's mouth the way a movie camera might, focusing on the sharp, pearled points of her teeth when she laughed, on the brief press of his brother's lips to hers.

When his brother pulled away from the girl, the light caught for just an instant a strand of saliva strung between them, and then they both raised their hands to their mouths, wiped knuckles over lips.

"Gross," Emil had said to no one as the other children swam to the edges of the pool and climbed out. But he thought of the kiss sometimes, at night as he lay in the dark of his room after his father had closed the door and gone. He thought of the kiss and felt dizzy and sick.

On the last day of school this year, he had finally touched the dark-haired girl's braids on the bus, and she turned around in her seat, fixed her eyes on him.

"Sorry," Emil had said. He drew his hand back and tucked it beneath his thigh against the rough edge of the vinyl seat.

"Don't worry about it. I know babies can't keep their hands to themselves." She'd flashed a wicked smile and turned away from him, pulling her braids over her shoulder.

During the summer, the girls' father came to the house to pick them up every Wednesday. He took them to the petting zoo or the movies, bought them lunch, and then brought them home again by five for dinner.

The Wednesday of the boys' week with them, the girls got dressed up for their father's visit. Mary Louise changed her skirt three times, and Rebecca stood in front of the mirror in the bathroom combing and re-combing her hair. Abby put on a denim dress and sat on the couch in the front room with the boys, the TV turned to cartoons and a box of powdered doughnuts opened on the coffee table.

"Where's he taking you?" Emil asked her. "Somewhere nice, I bet, if you're all wearing dresses."

Abby shrugged. "I don't know," she said. "We try to look good and smile a lot no matter where he picks." She reached forward for a second doughnut and ate it in two big bites, the white of the sugar forming a ghost mouth just outside the line of her actual mouth. Then she sat back on the couch and crossed her legs, brushed the dusting of sugar from her skirt.

It was late afternoon when the girls returned. Their father had taken them to the Science Center, and then to the mall for gifts on the way home, and Abby showed Emil the plastic necklace she'd chosen, a chain of shiny, colored beads that could be snapped together or pulled apart and rearranged. Mary Louise had picked earrings, Rebecca a new charm for her bracelet. The girls put on their new jewelry to show the boys and their mother, and Aunt Virgi admired the earrings and the charm, but rolled her eyes at Abby's necklace. "Oh, Abby," she said. "You always pick the cheapest, gaudiest thing."

"I like it," Abby said.

"Of course you like it," Mary Louise said. "It's kiddie jewelry. It could have come in a box of corn flakes."

Rebecca laughed, and Abby put the necklace in her pocket and went upstairs. She came back in a few minutes, though, the denim dress changed for shorts and a T-shirt. She found Emil at the kitchen table, drinking a glass of milk, and touched him on the shoulder. "Let's go play," she said.

Outside, they passed the pool and walked down the hill to the fort.

"Why does your dad come only on Wednesdays?" Emil asked as they walked. He'd been thinking about it all day. "You don't see him in between?"

Abby shook her head and said no, just Wednesdays, which was fine, because by then they were all tired of their mother, anyway.

"Doesn't it bother you, not to see him every day anymore?"

Abby raised her shoulders in a shrug. "Kids bounce back," she said.

At the fort, they stooped to enter, and then lay on their sides, their backs nearly touching. Emil traced the shape of his name into the dirt—a big E, smaller M, big I, tiny L.

"Why did he go?" Emil asked. "Your dad."

The sunlight flickered and dimmed, then brightened again as clouds passed overhead outside and a breeze shifted the highest branches of the trees above the fort.

"He and my mom don't love each other anymore," Abby said. "They're just like strangers. Like they never met."

"But they did meet," Emil said.

Behind him, Abby shifted, sat up. "They thought they knew each other, but it turned out they didn't." She let out her breath. "I don't know," she said. "I don't know why." She stood up and brushed the dirt from her pants, then ducked out of the fort.

Emil lay still on his side. His own father had left once, last summer, just after school let out. He took a duffel bag and a suitcase to a hotel downtown and stayed there. In the evenings, he called before bedtime to say good night to each boy. "How you doing?" he asked, his voice trimmed small by the distance. "How's your homework?"

"Fine," Emil said, though it was summer, and his father should have known there was no school.

On the weekends, he drove back to the house and picked them up, took them to the hotel with him for Saturday night. It was a long-term-stay hotel, each room equipped with a mini-fridge and a micro-wave, a television that got sixty-five channels. When the boys came, their father called the front desk for three cots, which he worked to set up while they watched. He smiled as he opened the metal legs of each cot. "Think of it as camping, boys. It's just like camping. Camping with a roof over your head." He ordered in pizza and let them watch movies until late, then took them out for eggs and waffles in the morning before driving them home.

While his father was gone, Emil's mother let him sleep beside her in his parents' bed, his head on his father's pillow. She hadn't washed the pillow, and it smelled of Emil's father—the stiff scent of his aftershave and the salty smell of his hair. Emil curled in beneath the blankets, closed his eyes, and listened to the sound of his mother turning the pages of her book. He could feel the heat of her next to him if he lay still long enough, her body warming the mattress and the blankets. He could feel her slight movements as she shifted or reached to the bedside table for a tissue. She didn't sleep and kept the light on all night. Once, when Emil woke from a nightmare at three in the morning, she was still awake, her glasses on, and her eyes behind them heavy-lidded and tired. She rubbed circles on his back until he slept again, just like she'd done to help him sleep when he was small. As Emil drifted off, he thought of his father across town in the hotel, and hoped he would come back home, but not too soon.

One weekend, his brothers away at camp for the week, only Emil went to the hotel to visit his father. They spent the afternoon at the pool and then took the elevator up to the room to call out for cheese pizza and watch the evening news. When the pizza arrived, they sat on the edge of the bed to eat, Emil wrapped in a towel and still wearing his suit, soaking a wet spot through the bedspread. The bedspread was shiny and rough, and his father rolled it back to the foot of the bed each night before sleeping. Emil traced the dashed lines of the quilting as he ate his pizza, moving his fingers over the broken stitches.

"How's your mother?" Emil's father said. He kept his eyes on the TV. "Is she crying? Have you seen her cry?"

Emil felt his face flush warm, shook his head. He wished now that his mother had been crying. He wanted to tell his father yes, she can't stop, and then maybe they'd get into the car with the duffel bag and the suitcase and go home. But he shook his head, and beside him his father nodded.

"That's good," his father said. "That's good she's on her feet." He sat a moment while a yellow sunshine floated across a map of the greater Seattle area on the TV, and the weather girl directed her wand to a list of temperatures for the week. Then his father stood, wiped his mouth with his napkin, walked into the bathroom, and closed the door.

Emil got up and went to the window. He stood in his wet suit and his towel, the taste of pizza at the back of his throat and grease still on his fingers, and looked down at the parking lot, at the gleaming, humped roofs of cars lined up side by side. Beside the lot, the swimming pool was an aqua square, bright as a sheet of tinfoil and empty of swimmers. He could remember learning to swim, moving in choppy, gasping strokes between his mother and his father at the shallow end of the public pool only the summer before. The frantic choke of water spilling into his mouth each time his head bobbed again below the surface, and the moment of panic he felt in that space between the two of them—his mother's arms reaching ahead of him and his father's behind. He remembered the feeling of wheeling his legs against the weight of the water, and then the surprise of suspension, his body buoyed by his motion and by the bubble of air in his chest. His last breath tight inside his lungs and pressing against the soft wall of his heart.

It was August before Emil's father came home. The first night, when Emil woke after midnight and shuffled down the hallway into his parents' dark room, tried to crawl between their sleeping forms and fit there in the middle, his mother woke. "You're too big a boy for this now, Emil," she said. "You're too big to be afraid of sleeping alone." She lay in the bed while his father carried him back to his own room.

* * *

It wasn't until the last day of the boys' stay that the older ones discovered the fort. They'd packed their bags and set them by the front door, and then Aunt Virgi sent them all out to play. It was a bright afternoon, the sky high and pale blue. John took out the bat and the ball, and lobbed the first hit to the far left, over Danny's head, so that Emil, startled, reached up, took a step back, and watched the ball pass through the cup of his hands. At his feet, the ball landed and rolled to a stop in the grass.

"That's it," John said. "You can't play." He stalked across the lawn, picked up the ball. "You're out of the game." He reached out and chucked Emil across the head with the back of his hand.

Emil nodded and started for the patio, but then Abby hollered out, "That's fine." She turned to Emil and widened her eyes. "We were going to the fort, anyway."

The others followed them down the slope of the hillside and into the ravine. There was a smell of ferment rising up from the ravine floor, green and yeasty and wet, and Emil could hear the creek's metallic sound, like wind chimes or dimes rattled in a pocket— tinny and silvered and flashing somewhere behind the undergrowth. Ahead of him, out in front of the others, Abby took long strides down the hill, not careful as usual, her bare ankles brushing against the leggy blades of grass and the fine-haired heads of nettle plants as she moved. She didn't look back at him, didn't say anything until they reached the dome of the fort, and then she stepped back, a hostess, and let the others dip their heads and step inside.

"Geez, Abby," Mary Louise said. "You told him about this and not us?"

"You been coming here all week?" John asked.

Emil stood near the doorway. The place seemed too small with all of them crouched inside. It smelled suddenly rotten—some of the leaves that hung inside and away from the sun turning, softening like old lettuce. He thought about the worms feeling their way through pinhole tunnels just below the dirt.

"It's because she loves him," Rebecca said. The others turned toward her, and she grinned. "Baby love," she said.

"That's right. Baby love." Mary Louise grabbed Abby by the shoulders.

"And he's got it, too," John said.

The others laughed, and soon Abby was on her back on the dirt floor, a sister on each arm, holding her flat and spread. "Please," Abby begged. "Please!" She kicked at the air, dug trenches in the dirt with the heels of her tennis shoes. "I shouldn't have told you about this place," she said. She opened her eyes and looked at Emil. He wasn't sure whether she meant them or him.

"You're gonna kiss her," Danny said. He had Emil by the shirt.

"A good-bye kiss," John said.

They had Emil by his arms and legs, his body slung between them like a hammock, and they lowered him over Abby, who kicked at him, her feet at his chest and his legs.

Emil thought of John's kiss at the pool—the long, tinseled thread of spit and the way the girl had turned her face away after, wiped the back of her hand across her mouth. He thought of his father's hand on the bare pink of his mother's stomach at that beach in Florida; of the worms wriggling and tangling themselves in knots beneath Abby's back and the dirt, bodies like boneless, eyeless tubes of skin. The light in the fort came in patchy through the tight embroidery of the leafed ceiling, spotting the floor, and Abby's chest, and his brothers' shoes.

Emil looked at Abby. She was crying. Her cheeks were flushed and dirty, and the tears smeared wet tracks down the sides of her face. When she met his eyes, he saw that something had shifted. She didn't look at him with sympathy. Whatever pact they'd had all week had dissolved into anger, humiliation. She turned her face away.

"I'll throw up," Emil cried then. "I'll be sick," he said to his brothers.

They dropped him, and he collapsed to his knees on the dirt floor, coughing, and sat back.

The girls stood up, and in a moment it was over, the older four bored and stomping toward the creek to catch frogs, Abby released to run up the hill to the house, and Emil left alone in the shadowed cool of the fort.

In another hour his parents would arrive together, tanned and smiling, the trunk of the car still full of their suitcase and a bag of gifts brought back for the boys. "How was it?" their mother would ask. "Did you survive the week without us, Emil?" Emil would let his mother put her arms around him. He would lift his hand in a wave when his father waved from the front seat of the car, and then would pick up his pillow and his overnight duffel before his mother could reach for them, and walk ahead of her out to the driveway. The week had been fine, he would say over his shoulder. He had survived it all just fine.

THE NURSERY

AFTER THE ACCIDENT it was decided that David would spend the winter working at the nursery, hauling bags of soil, doing the hard labor and the handy work as his mother assigned it. It was her nursery—Beth's. Thirty acres of land just beyond town, on which she had installed a series of crude, glass greenhouses and some raised beds, several small stands of pines and birch trees still root-bound in burlap sacks, and a pretty grove of Japanese maples that colored a flaming red in the fall. From the far side of the property the Cascades were visible on days when the fog disappeared, and from the road, the fray of strip malls and housing developments that bordered the town of Woods Creek could be seen. The town had taken over the woods it had been named for in the years since she'd built up the nursery, but the creek still ran at the edge of the property in the winter and the spring, a narrow, silty vein of the Snohomish River where she had taken David to play when he was young, his small hands hovering over the water, clenching in fists above the darting bodies of salmon smelt and bullheads.

He was seventeen now and short but stocky. On his first day at the nursery he wore a T-shirt around the grounds, even though the weather was cold, and a pair of muddy, worn jeans that he cuffed above his rubber boots. He woke up with the alarm, ate the egg Beth fried for him, and took a cup of coffee that she watched him taste and then douse with three spoonfuls of sugar and milk. This early in the morning, he had the look of a boy still, his eyes swollen with sleep and his hair mussed.

"You all right with this?" Beth asked him. She got up and took his empty plate from him, stood at the sink washing their dishes and laying them out on a towel on the countertop before moving to the back door for her coat.

"It's fine," he said. "I'm not missing much, anyway."

They walked together down the pathway David had made one summer between their house and the nursery. There was a fine icing of frost on the rocks this morning, and where the path sloped, he lost his footing for a moment, and she reached for his elbow as if to stop him from sliding. He shrugged away from her hold. "You got it," she said, and put her hands back into her pockets.

There was frost on the plants she kept outdoors as well, and as Beth walked, she stopped to finger the branch of a birch, touching the small buds where leaves would appear in a few months. "I think these will be okay," she said. "It'll warm up in another hour, and you can water them then. Just a little water on the roots." She toed the burlap ball in which the roots were packed. "Don't overdo it."

David seemed to be listening, and nodded at her directions, following her as she moved down the rows of saplings and listed the other chores he would have for the day: loading topsoil into the back of the truck and making the three deliveries she had scheduled; re-leveling the small parking lot with the gravel that had been dropped off the day before.

She took him into the one-room building she used as a shop. There were four walls and a window in each, and a peaked A-frame roof David had helped nail down several summers before. Beth turned on the space heaters, tugged the chains on the three bulbs that lit the place, then collected a pair of leather work gloves for him, a shovel, and one of the coiled green hoses he could use to do the watering. She handed him the keys to the truck and the list of delivery addresses, and he nodded at each instruction, keeping his eyes on his feet.

"Hey," she said, and put her hand on his shoulder. "You remember to be polite when you drop off the soil." She smiled at him, squeezed his arm, and motioned for him to get started.

All day she watched him. As she worked in the shop, figuring orders and organizing receipts, she glanced up and saw him through the window, his frame bent while he watered the line of dogwoods and poplars. Later she moved into the greenhouses to tend the stock she kept there—rhododendrons and azaleas, blueberry bushes and spirea, as well as annuals and perennials and several varieties of fruit trees. She clipped dead leaves from camellias and trimmed a boxwood back into shape, watered the flats of white and pink and red poinsettias she hadn't sold over the holidays. Through the cloudy glass of the greenhouse, she watched David load the topsoil and take off in the truck. In an hour, he was back and began on the gravel. Beth could see the packed muscles of his shoulders beneath the fabric of his shirt, the ropes of tendons on his forearms and at his neck when he strained with the shovel at the pile of gravel. She wondered at his strength, at how quickly it seemed he leveled that gravel and the single-mindedness with which he attacked the task, his body moving in deliberate rhythm as he dug the shovel's blade into the pile and lifted it again in one easy arc. He had red hair, like his father, though he wouldn't have known this, and his father's eyes, too—close and blue and sometimes hard in a way that made Beth feel quiet around him.

When dusk fell, David waited while she shut off the lights and the heaters, then walked around the grounds locking up the greenhouses. "Good job today," she said when she finished. She touched his shoulder, and they made their way together toward the house for dinner.

At school, David had been an athlete. As a younger child, he played in the town's youth baseball league, and ran track for a season in high school before settling on wrestling, joining the team. Beth hadn't been sure about this. She had seen wrestling only on television— the sort of dramatized play fighting that sometimes shows on tavern TVs on Friday nights. She had enjoyed the game of it—grown men in superhero costumes and makeup throwing each other against the walls of human-sized cages, beating each other with folding chairs while an audience cheered. It was funny enough, and she had nothing against wrestling of this sort because it was like a play, like a soap opera or a circus. Nothing but an act. She wrote David a check for the uniform and the team registration, and she went to his first match and sat in the bleachers with the other parents in the gym she remembered exactly from her own high-school years—the smells of floor wax and young bodies, the stale popcorn a girl sold at the gymnasium door for fifty cents a bag.

Two pairs of boys wrestled at a time on two mats laid out on the gym floor. David was in the second group, and when he got up from the bench, he looked for her on the bleachers, and she lifted her fist in the sort of salute she had seen audience members use on TV. David was smaller then, as a freshman, not quite one hundred and twenty pounds, and in his singlet he looked fragile—thin legs and scrawny arms, his rib cage pronounced under the tight-fitting fabric. The other boy was smaller still. David checked his headgear, took his stance in a squat, and waited facing the other boy for the call to start.

The boys put their heads together then, they locked bodies and pressed against each other, and Beth could see David's grimace when he turned for a moment, a look that surprised her, that at first seemed to be pain and then rage. From the bleachers, she could hear both boys breathing, grunting to keep their footing, and then David was down, the other boy on top of him, and the scorer hollered, "Time!"

Beth got up before the next match and went out into the corridor and bought a bag of popcorn, stood eating it and looking out at the parking lot. Inside the gym, the next match had begun, and there was the sound of other parents calling out their boys' names, the voices of the boys yelling encouragement to their teammates.

She thought about the look on David's face and the press of the two boys' bodies against each other, the way their foreheads had met, their noses close as in a kiss. The way they had turned their heads into each other's necks in a violent crush. She didn't like the other boy's look, his expression when he pulled away, as if he were eyeing her son.

She waited outside the gym until the evening ended and David appeared with his athletic bag thrown over his shoulder, his jeans and sweatshirt on again and his hair still damp with sweat.

"I didn't win," he said. He was a boy again, his face puffy where it had hit the mat, his eyelids heavy and tired. "I was bigger. I should've won."

"It doesn't matter," she said. She reached out and put her arm around his shoulder, led him back to the car to take him home.

Beth liked having David around the nursery, close to her again. They fell into a routine, and although whole days often passed without much conversation between them, she liked that she could raise her eyes from her own work and find him out in the nursery lot.

She left the house early most mornings, setting out an opened loaf of bread and a jar of peanut butter on the countertop, and a short note of jobs for him to take care of at the nursery. She put on her coat and tucked her yellow work gloves into the pocket, walked the short distance from the back door of the house to the nursery grounds, and began what she thought of as her rounds. This was the best time of day—not quite dawn, when there was just the narrowest halo of blue above the mountains and the nursery was still dark, the leaves of the maples beaded in small gems of dew and the buds in the greenhouses closed like the mouths of sleeping children. There was a certain scent in the greenhouses at this time of morning as well, not yet the heavy green odor of late afternoon, but the individual perfumes of the plants—the junipers and the laurels and the wintering roses, cut back to barbed skeletons but still smelling somehow of summer. Beth moved through the rows of trees outdoors first, tugging free any dead leaves, noting any changes in the stock, and then walked inside and began the day's watering there. David passed beyond the greenhouse glass by mid-morning. He looked up at her and nodded, tipped his chin in acknowledgment. She smiled and nodded back then, returning to her watering, dragging the coil of garden hose behind her as she tended to her plants.

In the evenings, she closed the nursery at five, packing the day's receipts and profits into a money bag to count at home and walking back to the house along the gravel pathways David had tidied during the day. She liked the way the evergreen boughs brushed against the legs of her jeans as she passed them; her jeans would smell like them later when she undressed and put on her nightgown before getting into bed with her paperback. She liked that time of day as well—the hour or so before falling to sleep.

David stayed awake in the front room, the television on, long after Beth had washed their two dinner plates, their milk glasses and forks, and had gone to bed. From her bedroom, even with the door closed, she could hear the muted voices of a sitcom, and now and then his laughter or a grunt of approval. She didn't mind his staying up so late because of this—because of the comfort in hearing him awake in the other room. She remembered what she'd said to her son when he was a boy: *You're my guy, aren't you, David? You're my man of the house.* Hearing him there, on the other side of the wall, Beth felt easy and safe, and she could read until her eyes drifted, could turn out her light and fall to sleep without trouble.

Over time, David had become a better wrestler—the best on his team—and it seemed to Beth that he was obsessed with the sport, unhealthy about it, in love. She rarely saw him anymore. He spent the summer of his freshman year in the high-school gym lifting weights, and running laps on the track outside, so that when he did come home—too late for dinner and without apology—he came smelling of work, his tracksuit and shorts stained, she noticed when she did the wash, the armpits and crotch yellowed with sweat. She started doing his wash in its own load, keeping her things separate, leaving his clothes in a basket for him to fold rather than going through them herself in what seemed suddenly too intimate a chore.

In the fall of his sophomore year, he wrestled for the team again, and Beth sat in the bleachers and watched. David always wrestled passively to begin with, waiting for the other boy to take him, to get him down, his back to the mat. But then a look crossed his face—perhaps only Beth saw it—and in the last seconds David reversed the fight, taking the upper hand. He wrapped his arms around his opponent's shoulders, twisted the other boy to the mat, pinned him. This was sneaky strategy, some of the other boys' parents suggested, but reversals became David's best move, and the coach encouraged him to keep at what worked, to keep winning.

The wins unsettled Beth, though—the cheering of David's teammates, the sour smell of boy-sweat in the gym, the animal noises she recognized as her son's when he locked another boy to the ground, when he knew he had won. At first she turned her eyes away when he wrestled, didn't watch—and then eventually she stopped going to his matches altogether. Beth had missed all the matches David won as a junior and the state championships that year. She'd missed the practice senior year during which the accident had happened.

"There's been an accident," the coach kept repeating when he called her. "It was an accident. You should come to the school."

Beth noticed news vans from Seattle parked in the school bus lane when she arrived. The bald man she recognized as the reporter for the *Woods Creek Monitor* and several women and men in suits, microphones in their hands, stood as near the gymnasium as the police would let them. They all seemed to be talking at once in a senseless discord of noise, and she had to push to make her way through the crowd, had to convince an officer to let her into the gym. Inside, the boys still stood around in their practice uniforms. A group of parents sat on the bleachers in coats and hats. A radio tuned to a rock station played for a few more moments until someone shut it off.

The boy had been taken to the hospital, though it had been clear from the beginning that he was dead. The boy's body was flaccid when they tried to wake him, his arms limp at his sides, his head lying at a funny angle on the mat, crooked and out of line with his neck. And there was no breath. The coach had got down on his hands and knees above the body. He had pressed on the boy's chest with the motions of CPR and had breathed into the boy's mouth for fifteen minutes while they waited for the ambulance, but there was nothing there to resuscitate.

All of this Beth heard from the coach several days later. He drove over to the house and sat on her couch and spoke to David as she made coffee in the kitchen and arranged a few Oreos on a plate. She hadn't been expecting him, but it was a relief to see the coach when she opened the front door—someone to break the strain in the house, someone to talk to David so that she could disappear for just a moment, relax enough to take her eyes from him and sit at the kitchen table listening to the coffee burble inside the pot. Her son had become a presence in the house that pressed on her, made her feel tight in the chest and constricted. He sulked and would not speak to her. He moved from room to room, getting up in the morning to lie on the couch, then returning to the bedroom to spend the afternoon in a deep, still sort of sleep that worried her. She found herself looking in on him every few moments as she had when he was small, standing over him as he slept, holding the palm of her hand close enough to his mouth to feel the wet condensation of his breath on her skin.

Once, he had awakened to her face close to his as she listened for his breath.

"Mom!" he yelled, startled and angry. He pulled the quilt up over his bare shoulders. "Get out of my room."

Beth stepped back. She felt as if the wind had been knocked from her. "You ought to get around today," she said. "You ought to get up and have a shower." Her voice came out sounding accusatory, and David looked away from her until she left, closing his bedroom door at her back.

When she heard the coach talking to David in the front room, explaining the situation, the school's decision that he should be suspended for a while at least—for his own sake—that he should take the free time to think about what had happened and prepare for whatever the other boy's parents decided to do about a lawsuit, she got up and put the cookies and the coffee and two mugs on a tray, and carried it out to them, smiling. "Coffee," she said, her voice bright. "You take coffee, right, Coach? David, I thought you might get yourself a pop."

"It's fine," he said. "I'm leaving." He stood, grabbing his coat from the rack, and walked out, letting the door and the screen slam behind him without saying good-bye.

"I'm sorry," she said. She sat, poured coffee into the mugs, and nudged the plate of Oreos toward the coach. "He knows better than to act that way. David has manners."

"He's upset," the coach said. "He should be."

On the other side of the front room window, David stood at the far edge of the lawn. He held his hands in his pockets and didn't move, but kept his back to the house, facing the line of spruce that made a boundary between the yard and the open field beyond it. He kicked his feet against the grass, and Beth saw chunks of sod upturn.

"I heard what you told him," she said. "I can keep him at home as long as need be. I run a business." She nodded toward the back of the house and the nursery. "He can help me out. I'll hire him. He'll be better off here, anyway."

The coach sat back against her couch, his knees open and his hands clasped in his lap. He took in and let out an audible breath, and then told her what had happened that day, before she arrived at the gym, before she came to collect David.

It was a practice match—boys from the same team wrestling each other to tone up their holds, to work specifically on reversals. The coach put David in charge and told the other boys to line up, letting David wrestle each one in his turn.

The boy who died kept fighting, though, lying on David, anchoring him. And when David finally moved the boy, finally got an arm around the boy's neck in a sort of clumsy chokehold, something happened to the boy, something within him collapsed. At first it was unclear what was wrong. The coach had been standing right there—he had been watching. He thought maybe David had just knocked the breath from the boy and winded him. But he was certain in a moment that the boy was dead.

The team blamed David, too; they might not be so easy on him if he was allowed back to school. The other boy had been popular. He had been in the homecoming court just a month back. He was liked. He did not have David's reputation for being distant and stand-offish, a loner.

David should stay home for now, the coach told Beth, sitting further forward and setting a hand on her knee in what she understood as a gesture of pity. They should get an attorney. They should wait.

Outside, David had disappeared, walking through the spruce and into the field where she couldn't see him.

When he was younger, Beth sometimes took him out to that field after school. David had a plastic bat and a ball, and she would throw to him so he could practice hitting. He usually missed, but now and then he hit it, and then would drop his bat and jump up and down, dancing in his silly, loose-limbed child-way across the grass to where the ball had landed.

On the couch, the coach replaced his mug on the tray and stood. "I like your idea," he said. "You could put him to work, just for a while, until all this is figured out." He smiled and reached out again as if he might touch her shoulder or take her hand, but Beth didn't stand.

"I think this is the best place for my son," she said. "I can look after him. I can keep my hand on him here."

"Beth." The coach looked at her, picking up his coat and shrugging it on. "I'm not saying our Dave's a bad kid. I'm saying it was an accident. I'm sure of it." He nodded, and she stood, walked him to the door, and held it open for him, thanked him for stopping by.

* * *

Beth could handle the nursery herself, keeping the grounds during the day and taking the books home at night. In the springs and summers, though, when the weather cleared and people began to think about their gardens, she usually employed a boy or two part-time, to deal with the new stock and the deliveries, and to allow her more time with the customers, who tended to want help selecting their purchases—help considering which shrubs would thrive in shade or sun, which fruit trees needed companion plants for pollination, how to take care of particularly finicky roses. The boys were usually David's acquaintances—teenagers old enough and responsible enough to drive the delivery truck and guaranteed to return to school in August. This last season, though, Beth had hired Uri and had kept him on for the fall and now the winter, not because she needed the help, but because he needed the job. She pitied him and his loneliness, and she couldn't see who would hire him if she let him go.

Uri was past middle age; she guessed around fifty—older than her by a decade at least. He was wiry and thin, and throughout his first day he smoked while he worked. At the close of the day, Beth found the butts of his cigarettes littering the nursery grounds, half-smoked stubs crushed between the rows of yellow forsythia plants in the greenhouse, the wet sawdust of tobacco spilling from the broken wrappers onto her dirt.

"No smoking," she told him the following morning. "I should have said before, but no smoking."

"You worried about your plants? Because I don't think it's a problem out here." He'd been shoveling and spreading new topsoil near the shop, and had dug the blade of the shovel into the earth when she approached him, kept the toe of his boot propped up on it, and leaned against the handle. "It's open air out here."

"There's just a rule," she said. "Sorry." She shook her head and added, as if to explain, "I have a teenager. He comes around sometimes."

Uri nodded. "I'll just finish this last one, then, if that's okay." She could hear him humming beneath his breath as she left.

After that, he stood at the entrance to the nursery in the mornings, smoking one and then another and then a third cigarette quickly, before his shift, dropping the butts there along the road. He insisted on a break before lunch and one after, and when he drove deliveries, the truck came back smelling of his Winstons, the yellow odor of smoke as heavy in the upholstery as it was on his skin and in his clothes.

He kept his blond hair long and pulled back in a braid beneath his baseball cap, and when he held still, Beth could see that his hands shook. It was a nervous condition, he told her once, but he promised it wouldn't affect his work. "I take medication for it," he said and smiled. "And now and then a little weed."

"You can't use that here," she said. "I can't have you coming to work that way, either. I told you, I have a son."

He looked at her—a smug look, like the half-grin of an untrustworthy boy. It made her embarrassed to have said anything, as if she were prudish, overprotective. "Gotcha," he said. "Good thing you let me know." He turned his back to her then, returned to watering the dogwoods.

Later, Beth wondered how he got the marijuana and pictured him parked outside the high school in his little red pickup, waiting for some sixteen-year-old to open a backpack and pass him a Ziploc. She imagined his apartment downtown—a one-bedroom in the brick building across from the bakery and down the street from the post office. There would be an unmade bed, a thrift-store couch, a stained coffee maker on the kitchen counter. She felt she could see all the wrong turns he had made even if he could not.

When David began at the nursery in January, Uri didn't ask any questions. There had been articles in the paper, but he didn't mention them. He simply nodded to David that first day as if he had been there all along. Later the two of them took their lunch together, David sitting on the opened tailgate of the truck bed with his thermos of orange juice, his peanut butter sandwich and apple set out on his lap, and Uri beside him, smoking. Beth watched them through the window of the shop where she ate her own lunch of leftover lasagna and a mug of fresh coffee. She had imagined David might come in and eat with her, that they would talk and joke in the easy way coworkers sometimes have; but she could see now that Uri had befriended him, that David would take his lunch outside. Beyond the window, David laughed at something Uri had said, nodded in jovial agreement. It was something crude, no doubt. Or they were laughing about her maybe, because she was the boss and the mother, the authority around the place.

Beth nudged the last of her lasagna around on its plastic plate, dumped it in the trash, and got back to work.

In the evening, fog settled in over the valley and hung low above the nursery, obscuring the tops of the taller saplings, clouding the glass dome of the greenhouse, and tempering the last of the daylight. There were no lamps inside the greenhouses, and so Beth looped the hoses into neat bundles and locked up early, gathering her coat and closing the shop before starting toward the house. In the distance, Uri's truck chortled and started up.

Behind her on the path she heard David's footsteps. "Hey," she said. "Walk with me." She stopped and waited for him to catch up so they could walk side by side. She reached out to touch his arm, but he stepped away from her grasp.

He had pulled a dark sweatshirt on over his T-shirt, and he smelled of sweat and of the air outdoors—gray and damp. Under his arm, he carried the cloth lunch sack he used to take to school, and he had to slow himself to walk in pace with her, his stride longer and more deliberate than her own.

"Good you're getting along with Uri," she said. And then, in a lighter tone: "Lesson one of the working world—making do with your coworkers." She tried to laugh, reached out to touch the bough of a pine as she passed it and felt its bristles on the tender skin of her palm.

"He's a good guy," David said. "You're hard on him."

In the fog, David seemed indistinct, even right beside her. "Well, I can see how it might seem that way to you," Beth said. "You haven't worked long. This is your first job. You don't know the experience of another boss yet, and you don't know Uri."

She listened to the sound of their feet on the gravel path, the crunch of the rocks rolling slightly and rubbing up against one another beneath the movement of their steps. Above them, the fog muzzled the dusk and drowned the bit of moon that might have already been visible in the eastern corner of the sky. The fog seemed to drift in wisps, to hang, nearly, from the low blue boughs of the spruce trees and the bare branches of the alders just beyond the house. Once inside, Beth would turn on all of the lights and put on the TV as she cooked dinner. She liked the idea that from the outside the house would look bright and warm.

David had his father's build and his easily flushed complexion, his red hair and his manner of walking, of holding his mouth a certain way when he spoke and of speaking only rarely. These similarities struck Beth—the pure products of genetics, no different than the way a pea plant would grow to so closely resemble its mother plant, leaves and flower and stalk all biological facts long before the seed had sprouted.

When she met David's father, she was young. She had left home after high school and moved into an apartment near the boatyard in Everett, worked as a waitress for a couple of years before entering the junior college to take classes in anatomy and biology. She had liked science in high school, the way it made the world seem ordered—a series of knowns one could memorize and count on—and also startling and lovely. She remembered a heavy book the teacher had kept on the back lab counter alongside the extra class texts and a dictionary. Inside were photographs taken by tiny cameras inside the human body. The lungs opened on a double-page spread, pink and netted in a delicate bronchial lace. Hormones bloomed in pink and green and blue like the crystals she had grown in Mason jars as a child. And the brain lay soft and gray on the book's last page, a knotted mass of earthworms.

As it turned out, however, Beth had no stomach for anatomy classes, and so she took horticulture instead, finding a part-time job at a wholesale nursery near the navy base and not far from her apartment, where she worked Saturdays and Sundays and afternoons once her classes had let out.

David's father appeared there one day, at the nursery, which was nothing more than a flat plot of land with a few greenhouses and a trailer that served as a shop. It was Beth's job to deal with customer orders, and when he came into the shop, Beth took him out to walk between the rows of birch trees and quaking aspens, to look over their stock and decide on his order.

He kept close to her side as they walked, and she could smell tractor oil on his skin, saw its black grime in the creases of his hands when he reached out to put his fingers to the plants. He pinched a leaf from an alder and rubbed it hard between his thumb and forefinger, so that the green smudged and the leaf tore.

"We'd prefer you don't," Beth said, and he smiled, nodded politely, dropping the shredded leaf, and moving ahead of her toward the pines. He had a heavy step, and his shoes left pocked prints behind in the soft soil of the tree lot as he moved.

Before he left, he asked her to dinner. She hadn't been out in a long time, and she nodded, flattered, and wrote her number down on the back of his receipt. When he called later in the week, she went out with him, and after dinner, they walked along the piers at the beach, then drove to her apartment and found their way to her bed. Next to him, Beth held his hand up against the light of her bedside lamp and saw that his palms were thick, the skin tattooed with oil and dirt. She thought of him crumpling the alder leaf, and remembered the way it had rolled in on itself, leaving a pretty stain between his fingers.

They were happy for some time, and then they weren't. There weren't fights, but there was often the threat of a fight—a silence between the two of them that made Beth think of things freezing, of the way a lake or a river expands when it freezes, and the way she imagined the earth underneath it must crack and fissure with the sudden cold, with the weight of the frozen water. She waited for a break in his stillness, for something explosive to rupture the silence. When irritated, he seemed to stiffen, the muscles at his jaw tightening and the warmth she usually saw behind his eyes flickering out so that his gaze turned stony and vacant.

As soon as she became pregnant, though, he left her. She quit her job and moved back to Woods Creek, worked bagging groceries at the Safeway, and saved her money, and bought her land.

Now, looking at her son, at the way he moved his body as he worked, the force of him behind a shovel, the violence with which he swung the heavy plastic sacks of topsoil into the truck bed, and the stern set of his jaw when he spoke to her sometimes, Beth thought of his father. She hadn't seen the accident herself, but she could imagine David beneath the other boy's body, struggling on the wrestling mat. She remembered the look on his face during that first match, as if he were animal for an instant, his teeth bared and clenched, and it was not a great leap to imagine him hurting that boy—wanting to hurt that boy.

The thought settled in her, and she began to believe it was the truth. If she ever mentioned it to David, she would not talk about it as a weakness or a sin, but would say that some things were simply beyond us. We cannot manage ourselves the way we manage the faults out of plants, hybridizing a perfect rose or a stronger, taller poplar. She rehearsed this conversation in her mind and believed herself to be forgiving in thinking it, even if she did not say it. Because was it not also her burden? Was she not somewhat to blame, having picked a father for David in the careless way that she had? Having allowed David to wrestle in the first place? She might have told him no when he wanted to join the team—told him that it was vulgar, boys on boys that way. That such contact seemed unnatural and would of course lead to something ugly, and maybe even to the sort of violent act David had committed.

Some things are beyond our control, she would say, and she would mean it.

In February, the spring stock arrived at the nursery: three dozen buddleia already beginning to flower; several lilacs and quince and deutzia; as well as flats of snapdragons in pink and purple and red, chrysanthemums, and impatiens. Room needed to be cleared in the greenhouse near the shop for the annuals, and the shrubs would be stored outside, arranged at the front of the lot where customers could see their early blooms from the road.

Beth asked Uri to come in on a Saturday, and she and David met him and began the work of reorganizing, moving the unsold winter stock to the far greenhouse and re-pricing it, bringing in the new plants. The weather had warmed, the sky overcast but white and sharp and glaring, and as the morning went on, Beth took off her coat and then her sweatshirt, worked in short sleeves and still felt warm. Beyond the greenhouse, she could see that Uri had been too warm as well, and was crossing the lot to the back of the property with a wheelbarrow of poinsettia plants wearing only his dirty jeans, his T-shirt wadded into the back pocket like a handkerchief. He had the sort of barrel chest she would have expected to see only on a much older man, his ribs distinct beneath his skin and working with his heavy breath. A cigarette hung from his mouth.

He had taken David out the night before; she didn't know where. After work, the two of them had stood talking near Uri's truck, Uri tapping a new packet of cigarettes on his palm, shaking one free. She watched him offer it to David, watched David decline and smiled to herself. But in the next moment, David looked up and hollered to her where she stood near the shop. "I'll be back," he said, and he turned away, and opened the passenger door of Uri's truck, and got in.

Beth watched them drive away before closing up the shop, locking the greenhouses, and walking home by herself. She made macaroni in a pot on the stove, eating it with a glass of wine in front of the TV. Outside, the light had gone out of the sky, and the homes up the valley were lit, small and distant needle-points of light visible through the trees. She got up and pulled on a sweater, stood outside on the front stoop and tried to listen for sounds of those other houses, but all was quiet. Beyond the edge of her land, there was the hum of cars on the highway near the strip malls—a sound that she might have mistaken for wind if the spruce had not been so still across the lawn. There was the gurgle of the creek if she listened hard enough, if she held her breath in her throat and listened past the noise of her own pulse. The cold water riding out the narrow course of the stream, eddying and swirling and wearing down the gray backs of the stones in the creek bottom, the muddy banks. The creek water slowly destroying its own bed.

Beth turned and went inside again, put the porch light on for David, and was still not asleep when she heard him come in, the front door unlocking and his voice saying something to Uri from the stoop before his figure appeared in her bedroom doorway, looking in at her. She lay still, though, and didn't acknowledge him, didn't lift her head when he closed the door again.

Today David worked beside her in the greenhouse, raking out the dead and fallen leaves from the winter stock, tidying the gravel underfoot, and Uri returned with the empty wheelbarrow and began sorting and settling the next load.

Beth didn't ask where they had gone. She dug her fingers into the soil surrounding an impatiens that had browned at its leaf tips and needed repotting. "Late night for you two," she said without looking up. "You must be tired." She lifted the plant and shook dirt from its roots, sinking it into a new plastic container.

"No different than any other day," Uri said. "I don't sleep. At least not without help. Sleep aid, I guess you could say." He smirked, and Beth believed she saw him wink at David.

She plunged her hand into the bag of soil she had lifted to the shelf beside the flower flats, brought up a fistful, and pressed it in around the roots of the impatiens. There was condensation on the dome of the greenhouse, water running in beads down the sides of the glass and dripping now and then on her scalp. "David sleeps, though," she said. "On a Saturday, it's all day sometimes. All day the rest of the week, too, if I'd let you get that way. You'd turn lump if I'd let you." She spoke to David in a cheerful tone, but when she looked up to meet Uri's stare, her voice hardened. "I'm trying to teach him to be responsible." Beth finished with the plant and set it among the others, heard David drop the rake behind her and leave.

Across the greenhouse, Uri laughed beneath his breath. He had the wheelbarrow nearly full, and he stood near it, shaking his head at her. His belly was flat and hairless, and Beth wanted to argue with him, tell him to shut up his laughter, but she returned to the plants, pinching withered leaves from their stalks, tugging browning petals from their heads, and lining up the plastic planters in neat order.

"If you think you should know," Uri said, "I took the kid out to eat. He said he hadn't had a burger in months, and I felt bad for him, trapped here all the time and almost eighteen. I took him to eat, and we saw a movie downtown, and then I drove him right back here where I knew you'd be waiting with your face pressed up against the glass." Uri set the last poinsettia into the wheelbarrow and pushed it forward and then back, turning around, leaving her in the nursery alone.

Beth brushed the dirt of her task from her hands, wiping the back of her wrist against her warm forehead. She twisted the air from the opened bag of soil and knotted it, carried it back to the shop.

At home that evening, she made dinner and set the table. David had come in from the nursery after her and disappeared into his bedroom. When she called to him, he came out to the kitchen, sat down at his place across from her, and began eating without a word. She had made spaghetti—his favorite—and had driven down to the Safeway for garlic bread and soda, for a gallon of strawberry ice cream that she would tell him about later, once he'd cleaned his plate.

They ate without speaking, their chewing and swallowing too loud, and the low voices of the radio David had left on in his bedroom audible from their quiet table.

"He took me to eat and to a movie," David said finally.

"I know." Beth nodded, and they ate, and when he was finished she told David about the ice cream, and he dished himself a bowl, and began toward his room with it.

At the doorway, he stopped and looked toward her. "You should be nicer to Uri. You forget he's alone, just like you are." David turned and left, and down the hall his door clicked closed and his music pitched suddenly against the silence in the house.

Beth cleared the kitchen table and shook the crumbs from their place mats into the sink, washed their dishes and the pots, and went to bed. Her arms were tired after the day of lifting flats, her back sore. When she lay on the bed, her shoulder blades against the mattress, it felt as though she were trying to relax a metal rod, and she had to turn to her side and lay with her knees up against her chest and her back curled.

She pictured David and Uri at a table at the Denny's downtown the night before, plates of burgers and fries in front of them, the cigarettes in the center of the table where they could be shared after the meal. Anyone watching would have believed Uri and David close, Beth thought—father and son, maybe. The waitress would believe she saw respect in the boy's eyes when he looked across the table; the people in the next booth would look for resemblance, and would think they spotted it, though all Uri and David really shared was the need for company. Beth understood this. She could see why Uri would want to spend time with her boy.

In the low light of her bedroom, Beth read from her paperback until David's music quieted in the other room, then she turned out her light and slept.

It was only a week later that the coach called. David was out with Uri—bowling, Beth thought she'd heard them say as they left—and so it was she who answered the phone.

"It's late," the coach said. "I should wait until morning to call, but I thought David would want the good news."

Beth was in her pajamas, her hair still wet from her bath and wrapped in a towel on top of her head. She tipped her chin now and let the towel fall and unravel itself, land in a heap on the floor at her feet. In the reflection on the front room window, she could see herself—bare ankles and drawn face, her hair wild until she reached up with her free hand to smooth it. "David's not here," she said.

On the other end of the line, the coach's voice was boisterous. "You can just pass the good news on when he gets home, then. The Fosters have had a change of heart. Their boy can't be replaced by ruining David's life—that's what the mother said to me. Beth, if you can believe it, that's the end of the whole thing."

The coach went on about the discussions between the school and the other boy's parents, about the wrestling team, about what David had missed.

Beth sat down. She rested the phone in her lap for a moment, so that the coach's voice was mechanical and distant and dulled by the sounds of the house around her—the washing machine churning a load in the laundry room, the heater kicking on and off. When she picked up the phone again, she said, "So he should be back to school, I guess. Soon."

"Monday," the coach said. "It's good news, Beth. You can both rest easy now and have a nice weekend." He wished her a good night, and she hung up. She sat with her hands folded and her eyes fixed on the frail mirror of the room visible in the dark front window—the blank television screen, the couch, her own solitary figure. She imagined Sunday night, David home instead of out, his sack lunch packed already and sitting on the top shelf of the refrigerator, and his knapsack slumped at the front door and full with books again. And then Monday morning. The walk to the nursery on her own.

Then there were headlights beaming in through the window from the driveway, the sound of a car door, and David stomping his feet on the doormat outside before coming in.

"It's raining," he said. His hair was wet, and he held a plastic cup from the bowling alley in his hand, the straw bent where he had bitten it. He looked up at her and smiled. "Good for the trees, though, right? Less watering for me to do in the morning." He shrugged off his coat and left it draped over the back of the recliner, walked down the hallway.

Beth went to the kitchen for a glass of wine, then moved back to the couch, turning on the TV set and staring at the news. When she counted forward, she figured only ten weeks until school let out, including spring break and the week of senior activities before graduation—a skip day when the kids drove into Everett to the water park or the arcade, a senior picnic, a day of graduation practice and gown fitting. So many wasted school days, and David already far behind his class. Even if he returned on Monday, he would need summer school, a tutor. And wrestling season was over.

Beth turned off the television and got up, smoothing the sleeves of David's wet raincoat and hanging it in the closet where it would dry. She locked the door and turned out the lights, and in the kitchen, she put out a bag of bread and two oranges, the bottle of syrup. In the morning she would make French toast. She set the table, folding paper-towel squares into tidy triangles beside the plates, lining up each fork and knife, settling the butter dish in the center of the table. As she did these things, it occurred to her that she didn't need to make any decisions tonight. All she needed to do was sleep now, and then get up in the morning and make her son his breakfast. She would get up early to cook for him, and they would eat together before walking down to the nursery. They would spend tomorrow working, just as they spent every day, and Beth could deal with the coach's call another time. This thought quieted her, and she finished setting the table, shut out the light, and went to bed easy.

There was a string of sunny days—skies blue and enameled and fragile enough, it seemed, to crack against the green tips of the highest evergreens. The nursery bulbs sent up shoots and then bloomed, camas and crocuses and hyacinths blooming beside the purple-black heads of tulips, the spotted tongues of the lilies. Beth ordered extra flats of petunias and bleeding hearts, pansies and primroses. She decided to try herbs this season as well, and so received a shipment of chives and basil, lemongrass and mint plants. A few of these she potted in oversized ceramic planters kept in front of the shop, where all day the sticky scent of the mint, the sting of the chive, drifted in to her as she worked, burning in her nose.

After a few weeks, she altered the daily routine, scheduling herself in the shop for most of each day to stay on top of the extra sunny-weather business, and keeping David in the greenhouses, to pick up the tasks she could no longer look after. Beth was pleased to see that he had begun to seem at home at the nursery, and that he even appeared to enjoy the work. His hands were callused and rough across the palms, and he had taken to buckling a carpenter's belt around his waist in which he kept a short-handled trowel, a spade, a pair of gardening shears. When business was slow and Beth joined him in the greenhouse, working beside him to trim or water plants, she felt contented as she hadn't in a long time. They rarely spoke, but Beth believed their thoughts were in line with each other, just as after standing side by side for several minutes, their movements naturally synchronized—David lifting his watering can at the same instant she raised hers, scissoring his shears just as she scissored hers. The easy rhythm of the work seemed to Beth a good sign.

"The two of us together make quick work of these chores," she said one afternoon. "I guess we're not a bad team."

"Yeah," David said. "I guess." At her side, he nodded and returned her smile.

The last Saturday in May, when Beth and David returned in the truck after making deliveries, Uri stepped out from around the green-houses, carrying a rake, and stood in front of the shop waiting for her. He tipped his head as David walked off.

"What is it?" Beth said. "Has there been a problem while I was gone?" She'd asked Uri for only a half a day's work while she and David made the deliveries, but still she had to pay him overtime to convince him to come in on a weekend.

He stood, leaning his weight against the slim rail of the rake handle and staring at her.

"What is it?" she asked, impatient.

"Your friend the coach stopped by," Uri said. "He was looking for David."

Uri let the rake fall to the ground at his feet and slid off one glove, searched in his jeans pocket for a cigarette, a lighter.

"Coach said David's missed his chance now. It's too late for him to finish out the year."

Beth looked away as Uri lit the cigarette and drew in a breath. "I appreciate that you're passing on the message," she said. "I'll have a word with David."

"Come on, Beth," Uri said. He held his cigarette between his teeth as he spoke, and Beth watched a thin tongue of smoke escape his mouth as he exhaled. Uri stepped toward her—close enough that she could smell the unwashed odor of his long hair beneath his cap, the scent of the chives he'd touched earlier still strong on his hands. "You can only control things so long," he said.

In her ears, Beth could hear her own pulse, and beyond her, the creek—a small torrent to match the rush of her blood. She reached up and struck Uri across the face with the wide plane of her opened palm.

Uri put his hand to his cheek. She had split the skin near his eye in a tiny fissure so that a skein of blood ran toward his jawline. When he took his hand away, there was blood on his fingers. He looked at her.

"I'm sorry," Beth said. She held the hand that had hit him close to her body, against her stomach, her fingers curled into her palm.

"You've never liked me," Uri said. He looked at her over the cup of his hand at his cheek, then crossed the lot, and got into his pickup, and drove off.

After David had been gone a week, Beth started driving into town in the mornings, stopping at the bakery across the street from Uri's building, where she could get a cup of coffee and sit at the wide front window before the sun was completely up, the light over the valley thin and gray-brown and limpid as creek water. Uri's truck was often parked in front of his building, but no one ever appeared to drive it. She imagined him and David lying on the dirty couch inside, watching television and smoking marijuana all morning, driving around together in Uri's little pickup all afternoon to kill time. She imagined they felt united against her.

One morning in late June, as she sat with her face toward the window, there was a hand at her shoulder, a tap. It startled her, and she spilled coffee on her wrist and the table as she turned.

"Well, shit," the coach said, and handed her a napkin, moving to help her.

"Thanks," she said. "I've got it."

He stepped back and sipped at his own coffee as she pushed the wet mess of paper napkins across the glass of the tabletop.

School was out for the summer, and the coach wore shorts, and a T-shirt, and sandals. His hair was uncombed. He pulled out the chair across from her and sat.

"So he's gone," the coach said. "He came to see me a couple of weeks ago. He said he was leaving." The coach shook his head. "He wouldn't be convinced to stay. He didn't say where he was going."

Beth nodded, though she felt as if she'd had the wind knocked from her. She touched her chest where it ached.

"I wouldn't have predicted it, Beth," the coach said. "All those seasons working together, getting to know him and you. I never would have pegged Dave as the kind of kid to skip out. Go truant just when he had the green light to come back."

Beyond the window, the sun slid behind a thin cloud, and the square of light on the table disappeared and then unfolded again against the glass. There were stone pots of begonias in red and yellow on the sidewalk that she hadn't noticed before. A matching set across the street, in front of Uri's building, and another in sight down the block.

Beth registered what she had heard: that David hadn't explained anything—hadn't blamed her. He had simply gone.

"I just thought he would come back to me," she said. "And stay."

The coach reached across the table and laid his hand over hers. "I wouldn't have seen this in him, either, Beth," he said.

She let the coach squeeze her hand, and then he stood and walked out, waved to her through the window.

Beth finished the last of her coffee, which had cooled in her cup. She looked once more across the street at Uri's building. She knew she would go on imagining David there whenever she passed. While walking down the street, she would believe she saw him step into a shop just ahead of her; she would turn her head too often, thinking she'd heard his voice. At home she would still hope each time she opened his bedroom door.

Still, even if he did come back someday, she knew now he wouldn't stay. And she wouldn't ask him to. Instead, she would touch his shoulder only quickly, and tell him as she should have done sooner that she loved him. Then she'd let him go.

ACKNOWLEDGMENTS

I am grateful to the many people who contributed to this book's creation. I am ever indebted to my amazingly hardworking and excellent editor at Chronicle Books, Jay Schaefer, and to the wonderful Gail Hochman, my agent, who first read this book in its roughest incarnation and saw potential in it anyhow.

I am grateful to Sam Ligon and Adam O'Connor Rodriguez at *Willow Springs* ("The Drowning" appeared in issue 56, Fall 2005); to Frances Kiernan and Sandra Beasley at *The American Scholar* ("The Nursery" appeared in vol. 76, no. 4, Autumn 2007); and to Hannah Tinti at *One Story* ("Familial Kindness" appeared in issue 101). Thank you as well to Joanne Brownstein at Hochman and Brandt for her kindness and effort in finding homes for these stories.

I owe an enormous thank you to my family: Paul, Dorinda, and Britt Sundberg, Marion Wilkie, and my much missed grandfather, Richard Wilkie, as well as the entire Lunstrum clan (especially Phyllis Lunstrum, loyal reader of even the most miserable first drafts). I am deeply grateful to Jacqueline Kolosov, whose editorial advice and friendship have been invaluable to me; and to Frances Hwang, Lily Hoang, Jodi Angel, Kara Larson, David Dodd Lee, Tamara Scott, and Ranjini Philip, who all read drafts of these stories along the way.

Last, but most important, I thank my husband, Nathan Lunstrum, whose contributions are too many to name; and my son, Finn, who had the good manners to enter the world the week *after* I finished the manuscript.